Bloodlines

Book 3 of the Wildblood

S. A. Hoag

Bloodlines: Book 3 of The Wildblood

ISBN 978-1-966538-04-2

9781793330963

Contents

Because there is always hope.

Chapter One

Black Hills evening July 1, 2058

"How many times have you looked down that road and wondered who was headed this way?" Kaden asked casually, handing the other man a beer. A warm summer night, and the Dakotas didn't have an abundance of those even before the war.

They sat on the porch, contemplating.

"I wouldn't try to guess," Harlan said, taking the beer. "Let's not." He considered the idea, then shook his head, deciding it wasn't worth dwelling on. "Do you remember the first time we came here?"

Kaden smiled, the memory a better one for him than his adopted father. "I do. It was snowing."

"You were four, and we'd been moving to make sure no one followed. The snow didn't bother you."

"By the end of the summer, you'd hidden a dozen of us here, more in other places. Seventeen years ago. After a while, I understood all the reasons you couldn't tell me."

Harlan shrugged. "The important thing was you were safe."

"It's why we're here now. Guarding the way north."

"Some things don't change."

"You can't stay here on watch forever." Kaden had a purpose in being there. His home was in the south now, in Colorado.

"I didn't plan on it. Then again, all sorts of plans went to hell in a handbasket over the past year, haven't they?" He wasn't angry. Knowing Kaden had helped the Vistans, even against the wishes of other clans, gave him a sense of pride. The outcome might reshape all their lives, but neither of them could stomach the idea of unnecessary bloodshed.

"You taught me the idea of empathy."

"I did. This could get out of control."

"More than it has? We're ready." Kaden had confidence in his people, in their people. The scattered clans were highly organized even with their small numbers, facts concealed from those on the outside.

"You don't want to get in to an actual war. We're trying to move past that." Harlan had seen war, up close and personal. He'd seen the residual effects, and the conflict might be unavoidable, as long as…

"Skolkovo," Kaden said. "Like it or not." During the last weeks of the war, two massive warships had moved into the Gulf of Mexico. Texas had become Skolkovo with little fanfare. The plague left few behind, and didn't miss the invaders, although they believed they were immune. One of those misplaces soldier had gone out on his own, and at the expense of Harlan and other unsuspecting survivors, set up his own enclave high in the mountains. Vance held the Front Range in a tight grip for years, until the Vistans blindsided him, in the dead of winter, only months earlier.

"Everything we hear is third-or-fourth-hand information. At this point, the smartest and safest thing we can do is let the Vistans take the lead. Skolkovo hasn't done a thing. I don't expect them to."

"We can step in later, if we need to," Kaden smiled to himself.

"You need to be careful where you step. The warlords don't have absolute say, and we're too scattered to make an issue, but they can go a long way in making your life miserable."

"Do you think they'll figure it out? Our Montana allies."

"That they should have stayed in The Vista? I imagine they know. I think they're too young and ambitious to admit they were wrong."

"There's nothing wrong with that," Kaden debated, being young and ambitious himself.

"Restraint and wisdom are a better choice. I speak from experience."

Kaden laughed. "Restraint? You?"

Savoring his beer, he brushed it off. They were all so very young, like he'd been. It was wrong that they had to deal with the problems started by men, governments, and corporations generations earlier. "Do as I say, not as I do," he recited.

"Yes, sir. You're not going to lecture me, because I'm advising them?"

"No. The thing about the clan warlords is, I'm the odd man out. The Altered are going to be more forgiving of you than they would of me. There's a line." He'd been aware of the genetically enhanced before civilization fell. They seemed to thrive in the aftermath.

"They trust you." Kaden could say that, being one, being an Altered and a warlord.

"And they expect I'm limited by the things I'm not," Harlan pointed out. They both knew it was true. Not Altered, not capable of understanding it.

"Fair enough. Now what?"

"We keep looking down that road," Harlan gestured. "Until it's time to stop looking."

south of Station 3, near The Vista, SW Montana
mid afternoon July 13

"Be aware," Wade warned his partner. "This meeting is not sanctioned by Security Command. It's a risk for you. There's not much they can do to me."

"You don't say." Mac stopped beside him, horse pawing anxiously at the ground. Trouble with their superior officers wasn't a new thing for the team. An old story, one they had become accustom to. "Could you pick a more conspicuous place?" They were within sight of the station, and even the horses recognized the area.

"I doubt it," Wade confessed. "Unless we went to The Junction, and we might. This is us, and they don't get to have an opinion now." It was a precarious position to take. He didn't care.

"They could pull support for this next thing you're doing. Jumping to Council six weeks after quitting Security. There's going to be a lot of hard questions."

"I hope so. We need those to make it look permanent."

"How long do you think you'll last?"

"Two months, twenty years. I have no way to tell until I sit in a meeting. Then the next one. Nothing is permanent. If they don't see that, I can't make them."

"A step towards being out in the world, but a step sideways rather than forward." Mac had seen him do it before. He had, too, by taking charge of the Cody base. Their Scout's demotion was a subtle move as well.

"We need to know the things they've hidden from us. The secrets Council has, the ones Command has. Ones they never intend to share with us."

"To protect us from ourselves." The fact they were Altered had never been a secret, to the three of them.

"They didn't want the war here. Delayed, not avoided." Wade wondered for how long.

"Fighting with them is old business."

"That's why I'm here. Command is letting it go on, for whatever reason." After he'd resigned rather than be fired for their venture abroad, Wade had time to consider his options, without the influence of his teammates.

Security Command, the ruling body of Vista Security, had been at odds with Team Three on various occasions, never so serious as this time. The team changed to compensate. Mac was sent back to the Cody base in what had been Wyoming. Shannon, while still a Scout, was driving less and sticking close to Station Two, right downtown in their home, The Vista, in southwestern Montana. Wade was team leader until recently. Unauthorized was the word they'd been told about the journey to Colorado, and he'd taken the fall.

"Council has been running over us all summer," Mac said. They wouldn't start on details until Shan arrived. She was unhappy with Wade, so she might make him wait.

"Did she expect me to do something?"

"No, she hoped Command would. At least I can get away to Cody. She's in the eye of the storm. It hasn't slowed her down. Sometimes I think she's trying to get dismissed."

"We planned for that possibility when this started. I'm not going to pretend any of this is a surprise."

"What aren't they telling us?"

"Shan might have a better idea."

"She has been more social than usual, going out to all the celebrations, dances, places her parents invite her to. You know, things she'd do, if it was an order rather than something polite, like an invitation. It made me suspicious."

"It should. She's looking for Altereds she didn't recognize before. I didn't ask or tell her to."

"Everything has changed in the past year," Mac said. "Especially us."

"I expected there were more here than she could see, because no one would go to the trouble they did, to watch the three of us for a decade. So did she."

"Do you mean Council, or whoever it is we're fighting out here?"

"Take your pick."

"I knew you'd say that."

"But the three of us are different," Wade corrected. "In all this time, in the ten years we've been certain, we've never found a reason, never seen others become aware, never found a trigger for it. They're here, even if we can't see them." Among other abilities, they shared a psychic connection. Each had unique talents as well. They didn't share details, except with a select few people closest to them.

"You can guess why."

"I have ideas. So do you, so does Shan. I don't consider it was random. We'll figure it out." He urged the horse on towards the gravel road. "Shan wouldn't come in from Helena alone, not this time of year."

"Are you so certain?" Mac asked. "She's not the same little girl that followed you blindly to Colorado last year." While their relationship was far from platonic, Shan and Wade had always considered each other siblings.

"A year hasn't made her stupid."

"If she comes in from the city," Mac nodded towards the decaying remnants west of them, "She won't be alone. You did invite other officers to the wake."

"A wake," Wade repeated, smiling. They didn't get to cut loose often, but Security gatherings were memorable.

"What would you call it?"

"A shindig."

"Wake." He wasn't particularly superstitious, but the anniversary of the ambush had been making him think hard about his life choices. "Team Three died at The Junction last year. Now we're something new."

"We don't need to go out there."

Mac shrugged. "Station Three is as private as we're going to get, while we're still within the boundaries of The Vista. It's the safest place for us, at least for now." Station One, at Anaconda, was too obvious.

"When do you have to be back in Cody?" Wade made small talk. He knew the impending gathering would be memorable. A bonfire up on the road, booze and food, loud music, speculation, and few worries about tomorrow. They needed the distraction, not just Team Three, all of Security. The Vista wasn't alone anymore. What happened a year ago had changed everything. It was time to look past it. If Team Three stayed, it added risk to everyone. If they left, it only lessened the risk. There were more Altered. Shannon would confirm his suspicions. Then it would be time to make a new plan, a truly new plan.

"A day, a week. Soon."

"How are things going out there?"

"Like we expected. When things go wrong, they go wrong. When they go right, we've got ourselves the base in Cody. It's hard work, long hours in the cold, our supply lines could be more reliable, but it's a good thing for us."

"We need to discuss Cody, but I'd like a few other people involved. You're in command. The final decision is yours."

Mac was quiet for a few minutes. A game trail they followed opened into a wide field populated by wildflowers in mid-summer bloom, and several dozen concrete building foundations. The station, three smaller out buildings, and the stables were the only structures that remained. The population had been less than a thousand, before the war. Now, it was thirty to forty people, at any given time.

"I didn't call you in from wherever in the outlands you've gone hiding, to not ask your opinion," he said. "I understand why. Maybe it's safer for The Vista if we aren't there. Maybe it's not. We need to remember to trust each other. You need to remember."

"The issue isn't trust. Flathead Lake isn't exactly the outlands. You exaggerate more than Shan does."

"You've shut her out, you blocked her. That's why she's pissed. Now, how are you going to fix it?"

"Nothing needs fixed. We, and I mean everyone involved, need to understand what's coming next. We need to be ready."

"For what?"

"Has Council tested their Rule of Law on Cody?"

Mac didn't have to think about it. "They did, once before we came back from Colorado, and once the week you went off to the lake. Both times were about their ability to impose their regulations."

"What was the consensus?"

"They were told Cody is a Security base, and that they have no jurisdiction. Until they can get a seventy-five percent vote of the citizens to change it, that's the way it will stay."

"They might try," Wade warned. "They might pull out the Gen En conspiracies from before the war and use them against us."

"But would they?"

"A year ago, I'd have answered no."

"These are our friends, our families," Mac tried to reason with the idea. "To most of them, we're still children." At twenty-four, he was the oldest of the team, born a few months before Wade and a few years before Shan.

"It's not about us, it's about fear. Fear of the unknown, of things they never believed, or they assumed died with the war. I don't feel they'd turn on us, but there would be questions we can't answer."

"We could find ourselves on our own, in Cody."

"We could," Wade agreed.

"Are we going to let that happen?"

"There have always been contingencies in place, and if things get out of hand, then the three of us go. It's time we reconsider that possibility."

"We don't necessarily go together."

"No, that's a discussion, a private one all three of us will have soon. The longer we're together, the more dangerous it is." Certain Altered were able to sense other Altered, and being in proximity multiplied the chances of their location being known.

Mac was the odd man out. His identity as an Altered was

unknown but to a handful of people. It had saved them, and he didn't plan on revealing the fact anytime soon. Or ever, if he had the choice.

"I don't think giving Shan ultimatums is a good idea."

"Do you think I'm stupid?"

Mac laughed.

"Have you seen her?"

"She was waiting for me when I landed."

"Shocking," Wade remarked. The affair between Mac and Shan wasn't new, but like everything else, that had changed.

"She's pissed at you. Again, or still. Give her time."

"We don't have a lot of time."

"She's aware."

Dismounting, they walked the last half mile. The Security sentry spotted them as soon as they broke cover, waving an all clear. A pair of teenage boys came down the driveway and led the horses into the stables.

"How long has she been stewing about my being out of contact?" Wade asked.

"Since last July," Mac told him, not wanting to get involved in the impending stand-off, and knowing there was no way to avoid it. "She knows you're keeping things from her."

"Not any more than I keep from anyone else."

"We need to sit down and clear up all the things we've been keeping to ourselves. That 'no one knows everything' mantra is childish for us now," Mac pointed out.

"You're right. Now that we have that cleared up, let's find our partner and figure out what's next. Is she here?"

"Your guess is as good as mine," Mac snickered, seeing great irony in the question. Wade and Shan shared abilities easily, and he didn't. They had grown up as best friends, and he was the first to join Security. That didn't mean they agreed on everything. More often than not, the opposite was true. While Wade was a natural-born leader, Mac tended to be impulsive. Shannon was the curious one. As a team, they had been unbreakable.

"Let's go find out. We have a lot of scheming to get to. Council might catch on and send someone to eavesdrop."

"Those kids? Secondary school 'potential trainees'. There are half a dozen of them, and a couple of guys our age, transferring over from the Caravans."

"So, the spies are already among us."

Mac nodded. "Welcome to Station Three."

Shannon paced the floor – it was what she did when she was bored, or deep in thought. This evening, she'd been alternating between both, waiting for it to get dark. She'd kicked the rookie running the com room out, Dispatch being one of the few jobs she could do without the constant reminder of Command watching. He'd ran off to find out who the Officer in Charge was. She was it, requesting the duty to keep herself busy. He could complain to the shift commander, and she didn't care if he did. If she thought too much about it, about what the day was, she might join Wade in whatever place he'd disappear to, and never go home.

Tonight would be a reprieve. A short one, no doubt. As soon as Command caught wind of their clandestine activities, they'd be recalled. Security had a superstitious streak. No one would be moving tomorrow. If she got the opportunity, she planned on hiding in bed all day and sleeping through it. Turning the portable radio to loud music, she set the board to switch off if an actual call came in. Then she waited to see who would show up first. Propping her feet on the counter, she leaned back in a chair, facing the door, and closed her eyes. It was early still.

"Comfortable?" Capt. Green asked, shutting off the music. "Can I get you anything, a bottle of wine, some hors d'oeuvres?"

"Do we even have hors d'oeuvres?" she murmured.

He pushed her feet off the desk, making her sit up, and stood against the wall, arms folded. He'd been her second, her backup, for a time, and knew what was running through her mind, even if he was as far from being a Gen En as anyone could be. A Blackfoot, a Siksika, he looked every bit Indigenous, dark hair, piercing dark eyes, in a word, intense. Born at the Ranchlands, a sovereign First Nation north of what was now The Vista, his tribe had been there for over four centuries. The First Nation had never been involved in the genetic experiments carried on by various conglomerates. What they had done was to keep the survivors of the last war alive the first winter they congregated in the valley.

"Are you doing all right?" he ventured.

"I'll feel better when they decide to show up."

"Wade?"

"I'm pretty sure he's been close for the past couple of days." She'd awoken to the beat of Boston, his favorite pre-war rock band. He'd been listening to them, wherever he was, and he'd let her hear so she'd know.

"Good," he nodded. "I meant, are you doing okay?"

"I am, but better Wednesday."

"Hangover Wednesday. You're on the schedule for a shift out of Station Two, so you might keep that in mind."

"I'll grab a car and go get some sleep, up behind the airport."

"You are trying to get fired," he decided. "Call me if you want company."

"I'm not. Scouts don't stay awake all three days of their shift. We drive a few hours, sleep a few, do it all again. Besides, you don't want to get fired either." Tall and slender, dark hair she wore long, brilliant green eyes, Shan was twenty now and quite aware how to use her appearance to bluff others. She'd been driving as a Scout for close to five years.

"The team went to a lot of trouble to keep the rest of us out of the cross hairs." He'd seen the struggle. "I won't be in Security for decades. I may not be in Security past the next snowfall."

"Go to the Caravans," she laughed. It was a running joke that the

Caravans sent their problem employees to Security, and Security sent burnt-out officers to the Caravans. Sometimes, it was true.

Green laughed with her. "Don't think I haven't thought about it."

"Probably every one of us is giving serious consideration to getting out." She meant the surviving seven who had gone to Manitou and brought down retribution on the rogue Altered that come close to killing off the team. Wade had quit, maybe, and Quinlen retired. Hunter was on leave and currently in Angelfire with a family he'd rediscovered. Shan's twin, Taylor, called Taylor One as there were two in Security and another in training, hadn't said what he planned to do. His brothers weren't her brothers; he'd had been adopted by another family.

Green, Mac, and Shannon were the rest of the group. "You've been spending a lot of time at the hospital, not as a patient," she noted.

"Yeah, I have."

"Instead of Capt. Green, should I start calling you Dr. Green?"

"In a few years, if I can manage it."

"That would be amazing."

"Here I was worried you'd be offended."

She sputtered pure sarcasm. They'd learned to adapt to their new world, or they wouldn't have survived. "In a few hours, I'll have an idea what I'm doing next."

"Things were a hell of a lot simpler, before, even if we didn't think so."

"We were clueless. As far as I can tell, we still are."

"Can we protect The Vista?"

"That's what we're going to figure out. If it looks like a possibility, we'll decide what to do to change things. It might mean we go out into the world again. It might mean doing things Council will consider illegal, and Command might have to agree with."

"Those are a lot of 'mights'. I hope the com room isn't bugged," Green said.

"It's not. I'm telling you for a reason."

"Because Hunter isn't here, and Mac has changed."

"Ouch," she grimaced. Her relationships with both men were well-known, and in turmoil. Her connection with Green wasn't public, or anywhere near as complicated. Team Three and their generation tended to not be monogamous. That wasn't the issue. "Because Taylor and I have been the ones keeping Wade in check, and you've gotten drawn in to that."

"Can you control him?"

"I back him. I'm the voice of reason when I have to be."

It was Green's turn to snort. "You, the voice of reason." Sarcasm. He'd witnessed it.

"I've never tried to control him, but the situation and we lost that a year ago. I don't see a good reason to go back."

"That's a dangerous thing, Shan."

"Wade isn't indiscriminate. He knows what he's doing."

"Then why did you have to follow him around?"

"Checks and balances. We're a team, we were looking out for each other a long time before that. It's a self-defense mechanism, because Wade saw trouble before either of us. He realized people right here are as big a threat to us as anyone we met out in the world."

"What's he been doing the past six weeks?"

"No idea. He asked for some privacy."

"If Council gets something on any of the team, you understand what that means."

"We do."

"If you think they won't exile you for those things..."

"The things I've found out about. The things we discovered could destroy what we've been fighting to protect."

"Like I said, it's a dangerous game. Be certain you want to keep playing. Council can be as ruthless as the outlanders we've crossed paths with. Will Command stand with you, or throw you to the wolves?"

"We'll find out." The com began beeping, lights in the room flashing to warn of an incoming call. "And there's that."

"Station Three, Car Eleven, dropping off a couple of guests for the night."

"Car Eleven, civilians or other?" she answered.

"Officers going on duty tomorrow, we won't be on the roads, so here they are."

"Gotcha, come on in. Alert Six. All clear."

"Alert Six," he responded, ending the conversation as another dispatch officer arrived to relieve Shannon.

"All clear," she repeated. "I doubt you'll get any calls overnight. There's no commander in the station, relay to The Vista if you need anything."

"Your brother invited us up to the loft for drinks." Green opened the door and held it for her.

"That doesn't make me suspicious at all." The loft was on the third floor, the top floor of the main lodge, a large, elegant room with an outstanding view of the mountains and a direct view into the main hall below. It was occupied by whoever was in charge for the week. Private quarters occupied the second floor; the com room, armory, kitchen, lobby, dayroom, and other offices were on the ground floor.

"You've always been harsher on Taylor than anyone else. Even before you found out he was your brother," Green pointed out, following her through the main lobby. The building had been lavish, a winter retreat, before the war. Claimed as a security station a decade later, it was reinforced, remodeled, and rebuilt for defense rather than opulence. It was still beautiful, with massive wooden beams running across the ceiling, spacious rooms, functional furnishings, and more importantly, well off the highway.

"Maybe it was sibling rivalry, and I didn't understand why."

Green stopped to speculate about that one. "Maybe it was."

"I'm curious to hear what he has to say. He has his agenda, we have ours."

"You don't think they're the same?"

"They never have been. Wade chose him to be his second. He's not working against us; it's more of a parallel course."

"Taylor and Mac fight all the time, and sometimes it's serious." They made the landing on the third floor, still quiet. It wouldn't be, later. A handful of people had arrived, gathered in groups to talk. "Whatever their differences are, he's still part of the 'Conda, and Wade relies on him," Green said. The 'Conda, the Anaconda Central Security Corps, had been created by Wade even before she'd joined the team. Their purpose was to support Security, in any capacity needed.

"Even if I don't agree," she noted, as Taylor joined them near the fireplace. It was made from Yellowstone River rock, and smoldering a low fire of cedar wood, purely for the scent of it.

"It's good to see you out of The Vista, for a change," he greeted her, nodding at her escort. "Out of dispatch. Where did you work today?"

"Dispatch," Green piped up jovially. "I dragged her out at shift change or she'd stay overnight."

"Not true," she disputed. "I planned on a hot shower, a bottle of rum, and a good book while I stayed in bed all day."

"It's not like you to hide. Are they here?" Taylor asked.

"Sure they are."

"Have you contacted them?"

"No, I don't need to. They'll be here."

Taylor looked around the room. "Do you see the officers who aren't here?"

"It's early."

"Fine," he gave her that. "Check again later, after Wade is here, after Mac is here. See what I mean, then ask yourself why."

"I will," she said. "You aren't as close to this as you want to be. I promise you, it's better this way."

"What has the team been conspiring?"

"Nothing, yet," Green said.

"Are you telling him to back off?" Taylor asked, meaning Green.

"I didn't have to."

"When we blew the side out of a mountain in Manitou back in January to get the sonofabitch that nearly killed her, I knew my time in Security was about done," Green said, voice low.

Shan glanced over. "We got him. He won't be sneaking up on anyone ever again. Neither will his cohort, because we know all about him now, too."

Vance, calling himself the governor of Colorado because of his position in Estes Park, had tired of cleaning up the carnage of his partner, Rafe. After the failed assassination attempt, it had been a simple thing to set both Team Three against Rafe, and with any outcome, Vance won. They had been watching the members of the team since they were children, and recognized a future threat. Vance plotted, Rafe died, and Team Three made a name for themselves along the Front Range.

"Point is, it isn't over," Taylor went on.

"We don't want any more casualties," Shan said. "I don't just mean from Vance."

"You think you can stop it all by yourselves."

"What we think is between the three of us."

"You're really going to cut everyone else out?"

"I have no idea what we're going to do after tomorrow. We are going to talk about it, if they ever bother to wander upstairs and join the party. Because this is a party. This is the anniversary of the last day we were a real team. Since then, things have been broken. We are going to try to glue it all back together." With each 'we', she ratcheted her voice up a bit. Shan crossed her arms and dared either man to answer. "That's why we're here."

"That's why we're all here," Wade repeated, Mac right behind him as they made an entrance. "Everyone gets an opinion, but Capt. Allen is correct. In the end, Team Three decides what Team Three does."

"Are we going to talk, or sit here and stare at each other?" Mac finally asked. They had locked themselves in the commander's quarters for a few minutes of privacy. Shan retreated to the alcove, pretending to watch the sunset. Mac was nursing a beer in a corner near the fireplace, while Wade paced.

"Who gets to pick the subject?" Shan asked.

"By all means," Wade told her. "If you have something to say, say it."

Sighing, she rejoined them. "What in the hell do we do now?"

"Do you want things to go back to the way they were?"

"That's not even possible."

"What did you have in mind?" Mac asked, intrigued. They had grown up in the same household, several families sharing homes those first years after the war. Resources were limited, food was scarce, it was colder than before, and, of course, the threat of marauders was a constant concern. Being Gen En, they were aware of one another's tiniest intricacies, even as children.

"You're in command of Cody. We need to make sure you stay there," Wade started.

"As long as you want to be there," Shan interjected. Once upon a time, the two of them had talked of leaving, traveling the outlands without telling anyone where, just to see the world.

"If I decide to get out, I'll warn you. We need that base, and I can't see that changing."

"Remember where we were at with our lives a year ago?" Wade asked.

"Point taken."

"Great. Mac has a job. They have me doing one scouting run a week, plus babysitting rookies in Dispatch. I'm bored, pissed, and about this far," she held up a finger and thumb half an inch apart, "from finding a new job."

"Don't do that," Wade told her, with something in mind.

"Give me one good reason, and not 'because I said so'."

"We've been in Security long enough to understand how things work. Not how we say it works, the speeches recruits get, the stories we tell to civilians. The actual work. Other than a shift commander, who runs a station?" Wade put out for them to consider.

"The teams do all the footwork," Mac said. "They don't have control over the station. Like right at this moment, one person does."

Shan took a seat. "I see where you're going."

"Straight to Dispatch," Wade said. "At any given time, the lead dispatcher controls the station. Someone in this room has been a qualified dispatch officer for five years and even was involved in a Blackout."

"You think I should move to Dispatch?" she asked.

"Too conspicuous. Keep doing runs, but lean towards preferring it. Drop subtle hints."

No one on Team Three understood subtle.

"You'll be on the inside, watching them, watching us."

"Oh, joy," she said.

"It's a good idea," Mac said.

"I know it is," Shan said. "What if they park me out here?"

"Take it," Wade said. "In the not-too-distant future, they'll reassign you to Station One or Two, because you have the experience. Either is acceptable." Perimeter watch was based at Anaconda, Station One, while internal security, Station Two, was downtown in The Vista. Station Three was more than a hundred miles east, for reconnaissance.

"This is all leading to what?" Mac asked.

"Finding out what they're still hiding from us."

"What are you going to be doing?" Shan had figured something was brewing when he left. The first time, hours after Rafe made his assassination attempt on the team, a year ago.

"It's common knowledge by now, that I'm no longer part of Security."

"It was a day later. Hell, it was in the newspaper," Mac chuckled.

"You're in the newspaper all the time," Shan added. "My mother keeps scrapbooks of us."

"I'll bet that's selective, because we've done some things moms don't want reminded of."

"Shush," she told him, smiling. He was one hundred percent right. They thrived on being together. They knew it had to change. It was far too easy for the other Altered to find them when they were together, unless that was part of a bigger plan.

"I know for a fact a council member is days away from resigning. When it happens, they'll call for a special election, since it's been more than a year, and the runner-up isn't eligible now. Command will express my interest to Council. With my resignation being so well known, I don't foresee anyone challenging me."

Both his partners fell quiet, surprised at this turn.

"Neither of you have anything to say? That's a first."

"Council?" Shan repeated.

"Can you think of a better place for me?"

She shook her head, "No."

"What happened with going to Texas, or finding a way to contact the Russians?"

"Once we're certain about The Vista's place in this, we decide when and how. We went out there blind before, and we paid for it. This time, we do it right. I suspect Council has had contact, but I can't prove it. When I can, we'll decide what's next. One step at a time."

"Great," Shan said. "You, telling us not to do anything rash."

"I never claimed to be perfect. What happened a year ago shouldn't have, but it did. I was wrong."

Neither of them had a smart reply. They sat in silence for a few minutes, listening to the sounds of the crowd filtering into the adjacent room.

"Let's go join the party before they make up more rumors about us. I mean, it is our party," Shan spoke up.

"The last time we were a team," Mac lamented.

"Yeah," Wade agreed. "Tell them whatever you think is safe. I trust your judgment. This time, it's our decision. No influence from Council or Command. Start saying that to yourselves, so we remember it when we need to."

Chapter Two

Station Three 4am July 14

Third shift kept to the com room, the only refuge in the station overnight. The commotion upstairs slowed and dispersed hours after midnight. A handful of people even made certain the bonfire in the middle of the parking lot was out at daybreak.

Despite their best efforts, or perhaps minimal efforts, it looked like there had been an extended riot of some sort. Dallas recognized all the signs as he picked his way through the lobby, not needing to check in because he'd be on duty soon. People were sleeping in the large chairs, the sofas, on the floor in sleeping bags, and there was varying amounts of debris scattered across the entire room. Sometimes, he forgot how young half the cops of The Vista were. Sometimes, he needed a reminder.

"Is this a good idea?" he asked the pair of men waiting for him in the kitchen. Cmdr. Duncan, in charge of Station Two, and Cmdr. Perro, retired. Both Security Command officers, both survivors of the war. This morning they wore civilian clothes, having coffee, trying to look inconspicuous.

"It's away from The Vista, the same reason other groups have meetings here. Besides, most of them are asleep upstairs," Perro stated. "We're right under their noses." He'd been aware of their clandestine meetings for some time.

Dallas got a cup of coffee – or what passed for coffee – and made himself comfortable. They had an hour before shift change would bring officers in looking for breakfast. "What's first on our agenda?"

"First," Duncan said, "members of Team Three are going to be asking how we kept them in the dark. They've already met today and the questions will come to us."

"We can tell them more lies, except now they know. They'll be looking for it."

"Or we can tell the truth," Perro said. "I see the damage we've done. We can't alienate them more than we already have."

"Are you sure?" Dallas asked.

"I am. What we need to be cautious about is how we talk to them, to control the chain reaction it's going to cause."

"Any of them, or all of them, could make the situation worse," Duncan agreed. "We saw how Wade reacted, and not one of us had any influence on him."

"His team does, his family does," Dallas reasoned.

"If we tried using his family to control him, it would be an act of war," Perro said.

"I never suggested that. I meant he listens, if not to us, to them." Dallas had stayed clear of politics since the war for a reason. Innocent people ended up getting hurt.

"We should approach Allen and MacKenzie as well."

"Yes," Duncan said. "Separately, or together?"

"Good question. Let's see how they plan to settle in for the winter. We'll cross that bridge when we come to it."

"If one of them comes to us?" Dallas asked.

"We get them in a room, all three, and deal with the consequences." Perro cautioned Command a decade ago about attempting to manipulate them. He'd sponsored each as rookies. He understood them as well as anyone on the outside could. Even after all that, he couldn't decide who was and who wasn't an Altered in the circle Team Three had established.

"What else?" Duncan asked.

"Council is becoming a genuine issue."

"Agreed," Dallas said. "They're pushing for a say in Security matters, and are trying to sway public opinion to agree with them. Every single incident, including the ambush of Team Three, has become common knowledge, full of scare tactics and half-truths." He'd witnessed a couple of recent Council meetings deteriorate into absolute chaos.

"They haven't connected the riot at the jail with the ambush. They could point this all at Team Three. I'm not willing to give them up, because you know it might turn that way. Old fears die slow."

"Have you heard any whispers about The Altered?" Duncan asked.

"No, not yet," Dallas said.

"There has always been speculation," Perro told them. "Nothing substantial."

"We need to keep Council out of our business." Duncan had a staunch opinion from years of watching the conflict.

"If they want a say in Security," Dallas added, "it's only fair that Security asks for a say in Council." All three men chuckled at the idea. They remembered the effort it had taken to separate the branches, a few years after the city was founded.

"Even at their best, I can't see a vote swinging far enough to let civilians run Security." Perro had been there from the beginning. Civilians wanted to stay oblivious to how their safety was maintained, because of the way things had been those first years. Out of sight, out of mind. It had been an advantage for Team Three.

"I hope you're right. First, they want a couple of Command positions, or run of a Station. Then they want Cody."

"There is evidence of incidents. If they go public, that will make people think twice about second-guessing Security," Duncan added.

"The remains of two helicopters are sitting in a hangar at the airport."

"Russian helicopters. They'll claim we fabricated it," Dallas figured.

"Like they fabricate stories about genetically enhanced humans hiding in the shadows."

"Except neither of us would be altogether wrong. I'm shocked we kept things this controlled for this long," Perro admitted.

"We'll get it back," Duncan assured them.

"With the delegations going to Angelfire and Estes Park, against the recommendations of Command, do we ask to have officers included?" Perro asked. "They expect us to protect their politicians, but not to express an opinion."

"Don't poke the bear. Let them have their meetings. Estes Park isn't safe for Security. It remains to be seen how our diplomats fare."

"A few weeks," Dallas said. "They'll leave before the weather turns if they can. Otherwise, next year."

"I'm sure there's a point to all the talk, and Council has been warned."

"Since Team Three is insistent about Vance and his city, there's a damned good reason. We're never going to get the details of what happened, but every one of them had the same warning about Estes Park." Dallas shrugged. "I read nothing good into it. Civilians are going right into a mess, or worse."

"Agreed," Duncan said. "And it's out of our hands."

Perro cleared his throat. The outer door swung open for a moment, and they were about to have company. "I didn't think this would happen today, but here we are."

"Capt. Allen. You're up early," Dallas greeted.

"Gentlemen." She looked around speculatively. At a glance, she didn't appear armed; wearing black jeans, black boots, and a gray button-up shirt, hair loose, half asleep. "Don't kid yourself into thinking this is morning for me, Maj. Dallas. Cmdr. Duncan, Cmdr. Perro. Is there anything I can do for you? We're a bit off the beaten path for a Command meeting." Dallas wasn't a member, but he tended to be in on a lot of meetings.

"We were having a private get-together here, for that reason," Perro said.

"I can check the doors later," she excused herself.

"Join us for a few minutes."

She took the seat Dallas offered, but declined the coffee. "What did you have in mind?"

"After all of this, we've never talked about you, with you."

"You had your reasons," she debated, not minding that they meant to discuss the Gen En. They might know more than she did. It wouldn't be a difficult thing, after The Vista had been purged of pre-war information on the subject. They were the ones doing the purging.

"It was for your own safety."

"Are we going to keep to the same safe subjects?" she wondered, voicing the opinion for the second time in a day.

"We don't have to," Perro said. "We'll see."

"Off the record?"

"One hundred percent."

"Go," Shan said, satisfied. While Perro might have withheld information from them, he'd never lied.

"I've heard things about Team Three," Dallas started.

"Sure you have. Dark, scary things you don't want to know about. I guarantee you, some of those things are true. Some of those rumors are absolute lies, and there are a few we started ourselves. Do you want me to tell you which ones are which?" Shan asked.

"The team has gone renegade, and that's why Command is sending you to different assignments." Dallas didn't play around.

"That's accurate. It's not that black and white, but close enough. For the public, at any rate."

Dallas groaned. "One more. Does the 'Conda execute outlanders?"

"No," she answered, wondering where he'd heard that. It wasn't from Hunter. Dallas was his adopted father and they no doubt spoke of things she wished they didn't, but that wasn't one of them. "They operate within the laws of The Vista. Anything else is one of those lies."

Dallas nodded, knowing that was the answer he'd hear.

"You asked," Perro said.

"That reasoning is why we've been careful to keep other officers at a distance. Or as much as we could. Even the 'Conda can't say they are aware of all our ulterior motives," Shan told them.

"Your opinion," Duncan said.

"My professional opinion is that no one else would get called on the floor, not by Command, and sure as hell not by Council. It would be pointless. What happened in Colorado was our responsibility, but some of this goes back fifteen years, maybe more."

"You're twenty," Perro reminded her.

"It doesn't change the facts. Facts we don't understand because you decided keeping us in the dark was 'safer' than facing the consequences of what we might be. It would have worked, too, if the other Altered weren't watching us all this time."

"Council played its part, too."

"They've had an ongoing truce with Vance, the Estes Park Altered, who has been waiting for an excuse to eliminate us. That's why Council was sticking their nose in the Security business of Sweeps every spring." The practice of sending teams out to survey outlying areas had been discontinued for the time being.

"What changed?" Duncan asked.

"Last year, Sweeps Team One went off the designated plan." She spat out the last word as if it tasted bad. All her life, she'd admonished Wade for attempting to plan for every possibility. Shan preferred to go with instinct, spontaneous reactions. What they needed was a comfortable middle ground. Team Three seldom compromised at a comfortable pace about anything.

"You went to NORAD," Duncan said. He'd lectured the entire

group once they'd returned, not that it mattered. The damage was done.

"We had no it was intruding into another Altered's territory. Even if we did," she shrugged, "in time, they would have dealt with us as the threat they perceive. Vance said it to my face. Rafe did too. I believe them."

"Council is still sending our people there," Dallas said.

"This information isn't in any report," Perro said. "Team members agree they are the only ones being targeted."

"There's the chance of collateral damage," Shan said, thinking of the last attempt made on Team Three. Their flight from Estes Park had carried an explosive device that detonated when they were supposed to be in mid-flight. They'd been in Cody for less than an hour. Three other officers had been on board. Command hadn't been told about the actual circumstances around the supposed refueling accident in Cody. Some might call it good luck. Leaving ahead of schedule on Wade's order saved them.

"Certainly," Duncan agreed. "Team Three has taken steps to minimize the chances."

"The problem with that being, we aren't the only Altered in The Vista. Far from it."

"We realize there are others. Not how many, not who, in most cases." Perro sat back, folding his hands. A challenge. "When you say 'we', who do you mean?"

Shannon smiled back, a genuine smile, not the facade she often wore. Perro understood how she had men in Security infatuated with her. Lovely, yes, and more, charismatic. That was what attracted them. Her mother, her biological mother, had been, too. Shannon got that from her.

"I'm not going to tell you. You have always been aware of what I am. Anyone else who decides to divulge that information is free to do so."

"We'd be more interested in hearing how you learned about The Altered," Duncan said.

Her smile changed, but she wasn't defensive. "I expect you to warn me if someone is sneaking around to shoot me in the back. Or better yet, you shoot them first."

"What does that mean?" Duncan asked. "I thought we were here to be honest with each other, maybe for the first time."

"We are. I'm trusting you with certain information because the team has fractured and I've lost that core of people that are close. The caches being supplied, even at the Cody base, years before any of Team Three was in Security was a giveaway. I think you were involved. I'm not telling you because I've had too much to drink, or that someone else said I should." She had their attention. "I would have a very good inclination, if I shouldn't be telling you these things, or if you were being less than truthful with me."

"You'd be aware if we lied to you," Perro verified.

"I can read intense emotion. If you're angry, or lying, I see it. Sitting here, you might get away with it, because you're not trying to kill me. We're all a bit more paranoid than we used to be."

"How do you know The Altered?" Duncan repeated. He had his own ideas after working with the team.

"What color is my hair?" Shan asked him.

"Brown."

"Just like that. I'm not unique in that ability, and it's not one hundred percent accurate. Meaning, I can miss an Altered. My perception has changed since we went out into the world."

"Changed how?" Perro asked.

"I sensed a few dozen Altered. Now there are more."

"How many more?"

"I haven't taken a census," she said. "I guess my point is, those who know aren't going to stand by while Council singles us out, and those who don't will be in for a rude awakening. The last thing Council wants is to bring the war here. At least, I hope it is."

"I'm certain it is," Duncan said. "We've all fought to make The Vista safe. Even Council's secret dealings had that aim. They should have consulted Command."

"Command has had a few clandestine dealings of its own," Shan reminded them. "With the intent of keeping us safe."

"True enough," Perro agreed. "You must have questions for us."

"So many."

"While we're being honest, you might as well ask. I'll tell you what I can."

Shannon knew Duncan was uncomfortable with Perro's statement. "Was the war because of The Altered?"

"Depends on who you ask," Duncan said.

"I have an answer. If I have to tell you why, you're not as clever as you think you are," Perro directed at Shan. "After the turn of the millennium, The Altered were never meant to live alongside humans. They were meant to replace them, or many of them. They were meant to be controlled. The process was already in progress when the legitimate war broke out and ruined all the grand schemes. The Altered changed, even before that."

"We weren't meant to replace everyone," Shan continued, having been told the story before.

"The elite and powerful planned to use them, for whatever means they needed. There were thousands of influential families funding, legislating, and hiding the Altered, at the end. They didn't mind if their bloodlines crossed. In fact, it was encouraged. The Altered weren't chosen at random. They wanted them to be strong, intelligent, adaptive. What they didn't expect was abilities that would evolve without prompting, and erratically."

"So, the answer is no," Dallas said.

"It's a subjective answer; they caused it, they didn't cause it," Shan said. "Back, when I was in my third week of Security training, we got a classroom lecture about how important it was for rookies to study the old law books before we started on the ones written for The Vista. Things change, we were told, but not as much as we thought. Life was uncertain before the war..."

"It's uncertain after the war. The uncertainty has an unfamiliar face," Perro finished.

"I knew you were an Altered, Cmdr. Perro, the moment I walked into that room. I've not indicated it to anyone until just now. You told them years ago," she meant the other two men.

"And you can't read our minds," Dallas repeated.

"Not exactly," she said.

"I am," Perro acknowledged. "I was altered by the Mid-Atlantic Group, and that means nothing to you. Quick history lesson. They were latecomers in the genetic engineering field. I grew up in a controlled environment, much like a gated community, with my parents and two younger brothers, none of whom were Altered. I was schooled for a military career. Sixteen days before I was to be shipped to a more secretive facility for specialized training, the war happened. Despite what is believed, the war in North America lasted less than a day. In that span, the bombs fell, and the grid toppled, right along with the seven regional governments."

"The flu had started weeks earlier. Until then, it wasn't considered a pandemic, it wasn't even unusual. After it mutated, people died too fast to keep track of, and to be honest, there was no one keeping track."

"How did you end up here?" Shan asked.

"My family was up north on a business trip in Ontario. If they had any sense, they stayed there. I stole an airplane from a tiny strip north of Boston and flew as far west, around the handful of mushroom clouds, as I could. I refueled a few times and made it to the middle of Wyoming before I ran out of luck."

"Is that where you met the group my parents were with?"

"It is. If you want to discuss the details of those few weeks before you were born, I'm certain we can do that another time."

Shan nodded. "We were right, thinking we differ from you."

"Yes. To what extent, I imagine, varies from person to person."

"Wide variations. I doubt they can be duplicated, or could be, even before the war. Some of The Altered are unrecognizable, from what we were, before."

Perro nodded. "So I've heard."

"You can't judge all of us, by one of us."

"I'm sure we've wasted enough of your time," Duncan put an end to the conversation.

"Did you hear what you wanted?" she asked.

"That you still trust us," Perro said. "Yes."

"I have a request," she directed at Duncan. "I'd like to do a run to The Junction after daybreak. Today."

"Two teams, at least two cars." He'd expected the request months ago.

"I'll have to cull the number of volunteers."

"No more than three teams. We might be off the roads today, but that's only for Stations One and Three. It's business as usual for the rest of us."

"Understood." The three men stood as she did. "We'll be careful. So you know, Wade is here. He'll be riding with me."

"You couldn't have surprised us less, Captain," Dallas offered. "We're here to see Wade, not you."

She grinned, amused they'd fooled her. "Enjoy your morning, gentlemen."

Chapter Three

"Are they doing all right?" Green asked, watching through binoculars. He'd parked in the middle of the intersection while Wade joined him, letting them have a few minutes on their own.

"They're fine," Wade noted, taking a quick survey of the surrounding area his way. Taylor was off-road, parking to the south on a hillside, a sniper position, just in case. Shan and Mac had gone to the turnaround.

The Junction was infamous as a crossroads for outlanders. Team Three had been ambushed there a year ago by a rogue Altered. Wade had been absent; Mac and Shannon, the ones caught. The aftermath led them far beyond The Vista, looking for answers.

"You?"

"I didn't nearly die here."

"I treated you at Manitou after the assault on Rafe. If the hospital in Estes Park didn't have talented surgeons, and Vance wasn't still pretending to be our friend, you wouldn't be here now. You're all even on the near-death experience. The Junction started it for us. It changed your life the same way it did theirs. Unless you consider the fact you still think you could have prevented it." Few people, even in his inner circle, would challenge Wade. Green was one of them.

"There were a couple moments when I could have changed how things are."

"Except those moments might have escalated our problems."

"Absolute truth. Our first goal, beyond digging for everything that's been hidden from us, is to find a way to work around Vance."

"You want to go to Texas."

"I want to. I need to figure out a way to do that alone. The reasons are my own. You don't need to hear them. Neither do they."

Green shook his head. "She'll never let you. Can you think of anyone better to back you up?"

"The problem being, I can't say when I'd come home. If I'd come back."

"You have family here," Green said, aware of how touchy the subject was.

"We all do, and you know as well as I do, they're safer if I'm gone. The outlanders fixated on me, not her. Mac, I don't know anymore."

"Mac has a different perspective. He figured out you weren't The Sixth in the team."

A lie. "Do you understand what a Sixth is?"

"As far as what Shan knows."

"She tells you things that make you a target."

"I'm aware. I let her talk anyway." Green put the binoculars down, facing Wade for the rest of the conversation.

"A Wildblood is an aware Altered, not subject to the training corporations forced on those they deemed their property. The reason some Altered are called The Sixth is that one or both of their parents were enhanced by a specific laboratory. A Sixth can be a Wildblood, but not all Wildblood are The Sixth."

"Then there's no way to tell if you or Shan are." Both had lost biological parents to the war.

"There are ways." Wade wasn't willing to discuss it, no matter how much they trusted Green. Shan wouldn't broach the subject, either, so it was a moot point. "That arrangement we had, if something happened to me or Mac? It's still in effect." When Shannon joined Security, he'd recruited Green for one of his many contingencies, being if the worst happened, and The Vista was invaded or team members were killed.

"I understand. How long are we going to let them sit there, drinking beer?"

"As long as they want. Tomorrow, we start again."

"We're going to be sick later," Shan lamented, being a bit inebriated.

"That was the plan," Mac agreed, sitting next to her on the hood of the car. They were both wearing body armor over forest camos, a thing they hadn't done a year ago.

"Kyle is watching us through the scope of a sniper rifle," she announced.

"There's a surprise. I'm supposed to fly back to Cody tomorrow."

"Yeah."

"Come visit me, Shan."

"You know I will. Hand me a beer."

Mac passed a bottle and belched out loud. "You're going to be bored in Dispatch."

"Bored isn't so bad. I have books."

"When we have radio duty together, call me up and I'll play for you." Mac played the guitar. It relaxed him, and it relaxed her, too.

"It's a date."

"Long distance dating. What will Hunter think?"

"Nothing. He's comfortable where we are."

"You two have scintillating fucking conversations," Taylor chimed in, thinking they might have forgotten about their open mics.

They both laughed.

"Ah, hell," Shan sniffed, wiping her eyes, "I'm not drinking until two, expecting some grand epiphany, throwing up, and going home. It means nothing at all, to be here."

"Why are we here?" Mac asked.

"Because everyone expects it. Taylor, we're going off the air for a few," she said, switching over.

Mac did the same. "What did you want to talk about?"

"I just wanted to be alone with you for a while."

He sat back, pulling his dilapidated cowboy hat over his eyes. "I know, I'm amazing company."

"You're going to fall asleep."

"I might. Nothing is going to happen this afternoon."

"I said that. You're going to not drink so much after today?"

"After today," he agreed. "I promise."

"Does it help, knowing what we are?"

"Not really," he said, then peered at her from under the brim of his hat.

"Yeah, I know." She meant the Sixth, even if she wouldn't say it.

"It doesn't change a lot. We made plans."

"I plan on being at home, in bed, asleep soon. I've had enough epiphanies, thank you."

"How about one more?"

"Oh, Mac, you don't need to tell me. If you stay in Cody for a year, I'll be shocked. Stunned."

"Are you going to Angelfire before winter?" Hunter was there with his rediscovered family. It didn't bother him that she'd considered it. As much as they'd made plans when they were younger, learning about their genetics had changed all that. He didn't want her to be alone.

"No. I'm going to sit in Dispatch, and dig around in the archives. Look for those missing pieces. We want Council to think we've moved on."

"We did," he pointed out.

"But we haven't quit. We're a lot more clever than we were a year ago."

"You remember what I said to you, the night Command busted us?"

"Of course."

"Still true. In fact, forever." He reached out, catching her hand and holding it. "Ready to go home?"

Shan was quiet, savoring the moments. Finally, she spoke. "I am. I'm ready for this."

Cody 2pm Aug 10

Mac had the shift. Dispatch was lined with monitors and half of them were lit up with various buildings from various areas around the base. They always made a point to watch the interstate. Today, it was barely discernible from the rest of the frozen scenery south of the former college campus. He was concentrating on a lot of issues, none of them urgent. Later, he'd be on the radio to The Vista. When he spoke with Command, he liked to have the conversation set in his mind. They weren't pushing him, but the lull wouldn't last. He'd be organizing further negotiations with Black Hills on his own.

"Anything moving?" Ballentyne asked, bringing two plates of food in with him, a late breakfast for both. Brunch.

"Probably, just not in front of our cameras." Mac took the plate and sat back, propping his feet up on the desk. "Trini cooking for you in the mornings now?" he grinned.

"Yeah, most mornings," Ballentyne grinned right back. "I cook in the evenings, but her food is better." He was on the verge of settling down, and they both knew it.

"I have a question, and I want the truth."

"Okay, ask. I'll tell you, if I can't tell you."

"As much as we've gone to all the trouble of pretending we aren't different, more and more people are aware. We could've been kidding ourselves all along, that they didn't. The point is, I'd like a hard-copy of us, of Team Three. A history of what's real and what's not. For posterity, I suppose."

"A good idea." Ballentyne tapped on the monitor. "Elk in the west football field."

"We should go hunting after our shift. Fresh venison is tasty." He got right back to business. "If I offered you the option, would you be interested?"

He considered before jumping to an answer. "What sort of compensation am I looking at for a job this complicated?"

They both laughed. "I might not recommend you to take over here if I get the urge to head out in the world," Mac told him. "It would involve going back to the beginning of The Vista. Anything before that would be conjecture."

"Once this project was caught up to current events, what would you want me to do with it?"

"Keep it up to date, and keep it to yourself."

"There will be some questions about what's left out."

"You mean Manitou," Mac didn't have to ask. "As far as I'm concerned, as far as my team is concerned, that incident remains unwritten. Put that down – omitted at the request of Team Three."

"I'll need to talk to people. Not all of them will be Security or 'Conda."

"I trust you to be as discreet as possible."

"Wade's mother is important. I don't want to piss him off by approaching her. You can ask him for me."

"Between you, me, and these four walls, Lydia Cameron is nowhere as damaged as she lets others believe," Mac told him.

"You know this for a fact?"

"Yes," he nodded. "First-hand account. Talk to her, and you'll understand."

"Can I get help with this?" This wouldn't be a short-term project.

"Who did you have in mind?"

"My partner. He's been involved with the team and the 'Conda longer than me. Honestly," Ballentyne figured, "I'm surprised you didn't ask Green."

"He may not be as objective as you. I have no issues with him helping."

"I'll try to stick to the facts."

"Throw in opinions and personal accounts. It shouldn't read like a text book."

Ballentyne nodded.

"Don't feel pressured one way or the other, on telling my partners. This is for me. If they ask, it doesn't matter. I'll share with them some day."

"Are you going to read it?"

"Maybe." They set the now-empty plates aside. "It won't be at the top of my list of things I'd like to read, not after living it. A different perspective might be interesting, but, ah, no, I don't think I will, at least not in the foreseeable future."

"That wasn't the only question?" he asked.

"No. Do you remember the old GMDS, the Ground-based Missile Defense Systems they placed across the northern tier of states in the late 1980s?"

"I've read about it in history class, like you."

"You understand the basic premise, then."

"Everyone in The Vista got a front row view of a warhead detonating because of it," he said, repeating the official statement on the incident. If people didn't have nightmares, he'd never understand why.

"The thing is," Mac tried to sound casual. "Parts of the system could be made operational, if someone had the knowledge and made the effort."

"I'll take the bait. Why?"

"Because we could run a safety net, of sorts, from Black Hills, to here, to up near Butte. Seven hundred miles of rough roads, covered in a couple of Dispatch rooms, all year."

"You think this could work?"

"I know it could. They already have a section running a hundred miles east, and it has been functioning at ninety percent for over seven years. I've seen it. I've watched a demonstration of how it works."

"Holy shit," Ballentyne said. "Now I know what you've been up to. So, what's the question?"

"If this works out, do you want Cody, or do you want to go to Black Hills?"

"I thought you weren't going to recommend me."

"I'm not, I'm asking you. If this conflicts with whatever arrangement you have with Command, say so. The way things are, I can send you anywhere you want."

"Does that include The Vista?"

"It does. Say the word."

Ballentyne chewed over the idea, considering his options. "I'd like to attach a couple of conditions if I'm going to be in charge here."

"Let's hear your conditions."

"First, I'd like to pick my own chain of command."

"Has Capt. Green expressed an interest in making the move?"

"The subject hasn't come up."

"Bring it up," Mac told him. "Since everyone has scattered, you are my chain of command. I don't see a problem with adding Green, or someone from higher in the 'Conda."

"Second, I don't want weeks or months of sullen silence from your team. Keep me up to date. I can figure out what to pass along to The Vista."

"I think I can arrange that," Mac admitted. "We don't do it on purpose, when we block other people out. It's a defense mechanism."

Ballentyne nodded. "Understandable."

An energetic woman with blond curls and dark eyes let herself in to the control room, carrying a carafe. She was older than Mac, younger than Ballentyne, and one of the first civilians to make the move to Cody. "I thought you might like some tea. It's chamomile, with mint." Trini smiled at Ballentyne, gathering their plates. "Commander," she offered.

"Thank you," Mac held up an old, chipped porcelain mug. "Are you going to go back home for the next class of Security training?" He'd heard more than once about her ambitions, but not from her.

"If I can get a recommendation. I don't think his counts," she nodded towards Ballentyne. He winked at her and Trini smiled.

"Sure it does, but I'll have them save a spot if you're serious."

"That would be wonderful. I'm serious, too, Cmdr. MacKenzie. I've been waiting for the right time."

"You have a date in The Vista, a couple of months from now. Before winter. I'll have the com officer give you a firm departure date when we hear."

She flashed another smile at Ballentyne and was off to finish her turn at kitchen duty. It was how they'd met. Some of the more menial tasks were assigned to everyone, in alphabetical order, and hers was Barnes.

"Thanks," he told Mac.

"No worries. I figure I owed you at least one favor."

"Yeah, I've covered a few for you."

"It's rough, having a personal life and being in Security," Mac said, both of them having first-hand experience to prove it.

"So, who's going to be manning this safety net?"

"We'll have monitoring stations, and you remember how well that works out in the winter."

"It doesn't."

"We need to get people trained to not only travel these roads, but to maintain and repair equipment that"s sensitive. Plus, being alone in a small group for two or three months."

"That's where Black Hills comes in."

"They can teach us what we need to learn. I'm going to go there and learn those things. If we can combine forces and get ten teams out, we can have it working next summer, not years from now. I need you here because you won't take shit from Council. They'll try something, they'll figure out how to interfere. It's inevitable. Plus you'll have our backs, come hell or high water. These things are all important."

"This was going to happen, sooner or later."

"It was. It's past time we take steps to keep ourselves safe. Security has the valley all wrapped up, but now we're aware of what's out here."

"How do we get The Vista to lend us some personnel?"

"We ask. When they see Black Hills is already functioning and willing to help, they'll be all in. It's going to put us neck deep in civilians next spring."

"That doesn't even sound like a bad thing."

"People from Black Hills will be here, off and on all summer. Consultants." Mac shook his head. "You're going to love this. The council of clan leaders for all the established cities are Altered. They call themselves Warlords."

"That sounds like some devolution for society."

"You saw what it was like in the cities."

"During the war? I remember."

"As things cascaded, the Powers That Be started exterminating The Altered. Most were kept in dedicated facilities, so it was simple. Hell, they could've planned it that way, just in case."

"For what purpose?" Ballentyne asked, surprised.

"Control. They'd lost it, and they knew they wouldn't be able to control The Altered on the outside. It's a human trait, to fight back. According to the handful of accounts I've been told, The Altered didn't go easy, and the survivors retaliated against the people who tried to destroy them."

"Another human trait."

"It is. The Warlords earned their name over the years. We will not cause conflicts with them. When they speak, we'll listen and learn. When Black Hills offers to be our sister city and create an electronic safety net for the benefit of everyone in the north, we're going to say 'yes, and thank you'." Mac sat back, waiting for a response.

It was minutes before he cleared his throat. "I've watched you grow up. I'm proud to have helped train you in Security. Now, I'm thrilled you can look beyond that training and do what's best for all of us. I think you've made the right decision. If they want my opinion, I'll back you with Command. Even if they don't want my opinion. Double that effort, with Council."

"We never meant to go out in the world, looking for trouble. We just wanted to look."

"You had no more choice in the matter than The Altered you've told me about. Sometimes, trouble happens."

"The purpose of Cody has always been to protect The Vista. I don't see that changing, but we can grow here, be safe here. We can do this."

"You had something in progress when you petitioned Command to get separation from The Vista," Ballentyne said. "I didn't know what."

"That was as soon as we got here."

"How long have you known about The Sixth?"

"We've known for years, someone was watching us. Someone affiliated with them, or Skolkovo, or a group we haven't crossed paths with, because we've been blind until not long ago. There could be a million people out east."

"There's not," Ballentyne said after a moment.

"I know," Mac responded. "It was almost a joke."

"Almost," he agreed. "What now?"

"We're going to turn the Cody to Black Hills corridor into a trade route that they talk about on the Front Range. We're going to make sure the safety net is perfect, and we're going to welcome people here with open arms. If they cause trouble, they're out. If they just need a place to live, we'll find a place for them."

"Noble aspirations."

"Yeah," Mac said. "If I'm so fucking noble, why do I have to keep lying to Command?"

Chapter Four

The Vista 8am Aug 14

"You look handsome," Lydia said, taking a step back.

~You look uncomfortable,~ Shan told him, standing next to his mother, arms folded, smiling.

"It's a swearing in, not a funeral," Wade told both women fussing over him. His sister, Annie, was in the next room, looking for a jacket that wasn't camo. Their youngest sibling, Nina, still in school, and being fifteen, didn't mind so much missing out on these particular activities.

"A first impression lasts."

"Everyone on Council knows me."

"But the public doesn't. You want to look organized and confident." Lydia brushed away imagined dust on his shoulder. "Are you wearing a pistol? No guns in Council Chambers."

"I'm not."

"I'll be sitting in the left side observers seating," Shan piped up. "Just in case."

"Do you think he needs a backup?" Lydia asked, out of the blue, as Annie came in. They both looked at Shan.

"I was joking, and no, I don't expect he does. It's only Council."

~That's what you get.~ Wade smirked back. With his hair tied in a ponytail, wearing a dark gray sweater that set off the blue of his eyes, and black leather pants, a new look for him; clean-shaven, neat, unarmed. "I don't need help to get dressed."

"You need help," Lydia said. "Or at least our opinions."

"I'm going to change. Leather is too hot already, and we'll be in session until noon." He left the three women standing in the hall while he retreated upstairs. His house, the big one on the western edge of the city, halfway buried in a hillside, hidden away from the main road, and well-fortified. In short, his castle. They had converged on him without warning.

"I'm coming to help," Annie called after him.

Shan waited a moment. "If you're going to talk to him before he's on the Council, this is the last chance you get."

"I'm not sure where to begin."

A mild sense of deja vu hit Shan. "Start at the beginning."

"The beginning of what? My life, his life, the Altered projects?"

"What would be easiest for you?"

"Not discussing this with anyone, let alone my son."

"You told me," Shan reasoned with her. "I think it's as important for him to hear this from you as it is for him to know."

"We're not weak. All of us who came here and created The Vista."

"No one thinks you're weak."

"Some of you talk about how damaged I am."

"We worry."

"Honestly, Shannon, sometimes I wish I was. It would be easier."

"I understand."

Lydia nodded. They fell silent.

"I can get the conversation started," Shan offered.

"We got blue jeans. Black leather is too sexy for Council," Annie announced, bounding down the stairs ahead of her brother. "Are you amazed?"

Wade was trying to be enthused by his morning appointments.

"They don't care how you dress," Lydia said.

"Come on, I'm your friendly Security Taxi Service today," Shan announced, heading out.

Annie excused herself, having an early date. Lydia took the back seat, knowing Security wasn't supposed to let passengers in the front. "She's going to your swearing-in."

"With a date. Do I know him?" Wade asked.

"He's a technician at the hospital."

They fell silent.

Shan headed for downtown, driving slower than she would without a passenger.

"Since the two of you have something to say, now is the time. We'll be in front of city hall in ten minutes," he told them, breaking up the silence.

"I've spent the past twenty-five years in hiding, protecting you," Lydia said. "I'll be damned if I'm going to let them ruin your life now. Wade wasn't your father's name, I picked an old family name generations back. Your biological father was Tomas Bianchi, and I met him in Sao Paulo. I worked for the government, The Allied States of New England. They had facilities in fifteen countries." The U. S. had separated into seven districts, right after the turn of the millennium, for corporate and capitalist reasons.

"His mother was Swiss, his father Brazilian, and when I met him, I thought he was another doctor working at the labs," she went on.

"But he wasn't," Wade said slowly.

"It took me the better part of a year to figure out the truth. He was brilliant and charming, and I never thought about it until the moment he told me. A doctor in biogenetic engineering, yes. He wasn't employed by The Sixth Consortium, he was created by them."

"The what?" Shan asked before Wade could. It wasn't something she'd mentioned in their previous conversations.

"The Sixth Consortium, one of the older corporations experimenting in genetic engineering, even before World War Two. I never looked into their history. By the time I realized I should have, we were on the run."

"The Sixth," Wade said. "It's a slander, now. It means an Altered whose parents were Altered." He looked at Shannon, still processing what he'd heard. "You knew I was a Sixth, you knew Mac was."

She nodded.

~Are you?~

~I am.~ She let it go at that.

Wade didn't. ~I wondered if you figured it out. Summer?~

~I imagine. It's not Michael.~ Shan was defensive, never having known her biological mother.

"Because of the intense competition between corporations, it could take years for information leaked to others. A significant number of Altered inherited aberrant abilities, before anyone recognized there was a problem," Lydia continued. They didn't have a lot of time to discuss years' worth of hidden truths and blatant lies.

"Did they consider all offspring a problem?" Wade asked.

"The variants began early on, but not all abilities became evident. Others were concealed. With good reason. Most dealt with their defiant Altered by locking them away, or eliminating them." Lydia remembered it like it was yesterday, nothing wrong with her memory.

"Variants," Wade said. "What sort of variants?"

"Things we didn't have names for."

"Things we have names for, that make little sense, but we understand," Shan added.

"Like ghosts," Wade said.

"What are ghosts?" Lydia asked.

"We can see events from the past like we are there. It's random, and it's often connected to a particular event that elicited intense emotion. We are the ghosts, intruding on their reality."

"You communicate without speaking," she stated. "I've known that for years. Is it all three of you now?"

"Yes," Shan said.

"You inherited the aberrant abilities. I suspected Geoffrey had, quite young. It wasn't by mistake that we all came here."

"To The Vista?" Wade asked.

Lydia nodded. "There were rumors of safe zones, scattered, remote. One near here, inaccessible in the winter, and certainly after the war. The Altered converged here, as they could. If they could."

"Rock Creek."

"Yes."

"Security has had it sealed up for years, in case of an emergency."

"Why are some of us aware, but most aren't?" Shan asked.

"The vast majority of engineered changes were benign. Parents chosen from elite groupings for specific traits; prominent physical capabilities, high intelligence, certain aptitudes, other political and financial parameters. Many of The Altered were, still are, unaware. A few individuals showed unique abilities and were isolated as soon as it was discovered. Sometimes we could rescue them. Those of us intent on keeping The Altered an urban legend are called Haven. We concluded isolation from other Altered stifled awareness, while proximity expanded it."

~There's the reason Vance kept throwing the word at us, and expecting a reaction,~ Wade told Shan. ~He claimed to have created the safe havens and wanted us to join them.~

~Lies,~ Shan said.

"So an aberration is the reason we are what we are." Wade would be able to deal with that, since it wasn't entirely a surprise.

"It is. They tried to replicate those traits, with zero success."

"What about your grandchildren?" His three children.

"They have a slight chance of inheriting an aberration. Traits are recessive as far as any of our research determined."

"They haven't," Shan spoke up. "I'd be aware. One of my 'aberrations' is sensing other Altered." She stopped on the corner and waited, the next turn being a block from city hall. No other traffic this time of day.

"Good," Lydia said. "You imprinted on Geoffrey early that he was your brother. I suppose because your actual brother was growing up in the same house, and no one would say it. Another lie, for your own good."

"How did I have a twin who isn't Altered?"

"A safety, an offset. It was a rare thing to involve a twin."

"Why?"

"Twins share a natural empathy. The laboratories wanted clinical, calculating, and obedient Altered."

"None of those things are natural to humans."

"It posed endless problems, even before the aberrations became obvious. Why they did it was on the whim of the Chief of Staff at the particular time. There was a lot of pressure to expand the experiments towards the end."

"Can we call it something other than 'aberration'?" Shan asked.

"We could call it Wildblood," Wade offered.

"I've never heard that," Lydia said.

"We have," Shan said. "It's another slur. Pretty much everything they call us is."

"A Wildblood is an Altered without the forced training," Wade explained.

"It seems damned accurate," Lydia offered. "Wild, rather than tamed."

Shan stifled a grin. Wade rarely swore, but after having spent time with Lydia, she knew it wasn't a learned habit from his mother.

"We refer to our abilities. It's a catch-all word, a safe word even in mixed company," he said.

Lydia nodded. "Rock Creek drew us here. We weren't alone in knowing about it."

"Do we have enemies here?"

"There are factions. We never determined what their goals would be if the Altered presence was made public. The consensus among Haven in The Vista is that, yes, they would be your enemies. You've seen what fear does, and it's not entirely unfounded."

"If they think I'm an Altered, why did they let me on the Council?"

"They don't have particular suspicions about you, although I'm certain they did when you went into Security Command so young. That follows, for anyone going to Command, or Council, or any position of authority. They watch everyone and tend to concentrate on newcomers. The thing is, they don't understand what they're looking for."

"Would they be capable of using an Altered to uncover other Altered?" Shan asked.

"I think they're capable of anything."

Wade and Shannon exchanged glances. "That's as clear a warning as we're ever going to hear," he decided.

"You understand now, you deserve to know what you might face. Some contingencies Security has taken up were started by Haven. There are others, ones I designed to protect my grandchildren, and others too young to understand."

"I wondered where that meticulous planning came from," Shan nudged him with her elbow.

"Dig yourselves in, at Cody," Lydia told them. "Don't let Command or anyone else stop you. Warn Alex." Mac, to everyone but the parents and Shan.

"Is Command going to be a problem?"

"No. They've helped us in different capacities from the very beginning of The Vista. You've made enemies out in the world. Council is about to begin diplomatic relations with your enemies. Be aware of those ties."

"It's our word against theirs, and they can't prove a thing."

"No, they can't, but it will draw the attention of the exact people you don't want scrutinizing you. It will create suspicion."

"So what do we do?"

"You stall the delegation to Estes Park if you can. Tell them what you found out there. Don't gloss it over. In fact, embellish the story if you have to. Do it now."

"Scare them," Shan added, pulling the car on around to park close to city hall, but not right out front.

"That won't be difficult," Wade said.

"Be careful," she gave them a last bit of advice. "The Altered, out there in the world, the ones not like you, were trained to be cold-blooded, to see other Altered as a threat. Never turn your back on one."

"Your mother convinced us to lie to Council, to break the oaths you're about to take, and to get ready to run to Cody, all inside ten minutes," Shan pointed out, waiting for her to disappear in unre-markable building.

"She did. Warn Mac. I'm going to make this thing with Council work as long as I can. We need any advantage we can hold on to. Get permission from Command to talk about the helicopters, about the tanks, about anything that doesn't tie us to Vance."

"Tell them about Texas."

"Yeah. As a last resort, we tell them about Texas."

———

"How did you get shanghaied into working this duty, Shan?" Kyle asked, standing near the fence separating the field from the rest of the school grounds. A graduating class of fifteen- and sixteen-year-old students was a few minutes from filing out to be recognized, in front of a thousand citizens of The Vista. The first of September, rather than the first of June, was one of those things that had changed after the war.

"How do I always end up like this?" she sighed, not upset, but playing along.

"Someone asked."

Shan nodded. "Someone asked to switch shifts, and here I am." A sunny afternoon, but the chill in the air had hung on longer; snow on the peaks from the first storm of the season, two weeks ago. It was early winter, without a doubt. They both wore white camos with full gear. Just in case. "Do you remember our graduation?"

"Not that long ago," Taylor snorted.

"But do you remember what it was like in school?"

"Sure. Tedious for me, boring for you."

"That's school for everyone, I imagine. Even then, we didn't quite fit in."

Taylor nodded. "You mean you, Wade, and Mac."

"Yeah." A group of teenagers clamored by, laughing and talking. A couple of boys smiled at Shan, and she waited for them to pass. "You could see it, too?"

"I had enough of my own teen angst problems to not be worried about yours." They started walking the fence line, keeping eyes on the crowd. Security let the celebration parties go on, their presence reminding everyone to keep it safe.

Did you understand why?"

"About the Gen En, no. A year later, the Blackout happened, and I'd known for a month, maybe two by then. I was told you were my sister, sometime around our fourteenth birthday."

"I've heard."

"Don't get mad at Wade all over again."

"Sure," she grimaced. It annoyed her that he'd constructed an elaborate lie to cover another lie their parents told. "We can blend into a crowd easily enough. We do it all the time. The thing is, we're more comfortable standing back, away from those crowds."

"An effect of what you are?"

"A result. We disguised our differences. The others, the unaware ones, they don't have this particular social malady."

"By the time we graduated, you were in Security already. The superintendent called you up for an award."

Shan groaned and rolled her eyes. "I was never part of any clique. I never wanted to be, and my feelings weren't hurt."

"Security was your clique as soon as Mac started training."

"I was ten."

"And they knew you'd be right there, along with Wade." Taylor flicked a cigarette butt away. "Perro started recruiting anyone from our household the minute we moved from grade school to secondary school, but he was watching us even earlier."

"They didn't isolate us. We did. Not on purpose, at first. As we figured out how different we were, we realized it was a good decision."

"Do you regret it? Not having friends who aren't cops?"

"I have nothing to base a regret on. Everyone I know is in Security, or related to someone in Security." Shan shook her head. The teenagers waiting, marched across the grounds and took seats in front of the spectators. She watched.

"You heading out to Station Three this late?"

"Yeah, the roads are clear. Travelers are settling in for the season."

He looked sideways at her, having gotten good at judging her response. They'd been circling each other for over a year, the unspoken things, that they weren't working towards the same goals. Maybe they never had been. "What are you expecting for the season?"

"I think saying 'I don't know' isn't viable. We spent years saying it and meaning it. Now we've learned about things."

"A few things."

"We're aware of what our isolation did. I have no specific plans for the winter, but I want to transfer out to Cody soon, then Angelfire in the spring. Hunter wants to spend time, and I'm going with him."

"Hell of a good place to be doing recon from," Taylor said.

"True enough. My plans don't extend out that far. That means I haven't considered what I'll be doing after the first of the year; if I'll be working for Command, or running away from home. If you're curious about what Mac is doing, ask him. I'm pretty sure you've asked Wade."

"I got a similar answer."

"Which made you suspicious," she figured.

"Wouldn't you be? The team is up to something, and you're not going to tell me what."

Why are we having the conversation, then?"

"For you to deny it."

"There is no team. Anything I do is on my own. I'm free to come and go as I please, and I have every intention of spending time with Hunter."

"Hunter," he repeated.

"Not Mac. I love him, I will forever. We both understand why we can't have what they call a normal life, or even a relationship. It's better if we're in different places. I've met people whose parents were both Altered. What I can see in them is... scary."

Taylor nodded. "Kaden."

"You brought him right into The Vista."

"He cleared all our safety regulations and quarantines."

"So did Rafe."

"This was three years ago."

Shan suspected they'd been infiltrated by Altered from the outside, and she'd even voiced her opinion to Command. Wade didn't dismiss the idea, but he hadn't pursued it either. "Did you know what he was?"

"Not until you went out and found him in Colorado."

"Right under our noses. I doubt he was the first."

"You and Mac had made the decision before you met Kaden."

"We had. Don't be thinking Hunter is who I settled for. That's not what it is."

"I'd never try to second-guess you on the men you chose to spend time with," Taylor defended himself.

"Then why do you hate Mac so much?"

"Hate is a strong word," he said, knowing why, and in the same instant, knowing she could pick it from his thoughts. It happened more between them than others, and it wasn't exactly reading his mind. It wasn't exactly not reading his mind, either.

Shan didn't say a thing about the stray thought. "Pretty damned strong dislike, then." She squinted against the setting sun, watching the students file along to shake hands with the teachers. Four years ago, they had been the ones marching across the stage. Uncomfortable and embarrassing for her, and the same for them.

"You knew," he said, the accusation obvious.

"You're going to have to be more specific," she parried, deflecting.

"Mac, and what happened the year he was a rookie."

Shannon peered back at him. "At twelve, I didn't give a shit about what Mac was doing with girls."

"How did you find out?"

"How?" she asked, as if it were painfully obvious. "He had nothing else on his mind for months. The Blackout pulled him out of it."

Taylor looked skeptical. She'd played that trick before, pretending she knew something, to get him to confess all.

"Oh, seriously Kyle, fuck off. I became aware of her and the baby. And again, I didn't care."

"Not then," he said. "After a few years, it bothered you. It still does."

"Of course it does," Shan spat out. "Is that what you want to hear? Do you want to know how I feel about having to pretend it doesn't hurt? Why do you think he's in Cody and I'm not?" Her breath caught.

"I'm sorry."

"He'd been telling me for years what mixing our already altered genetics might do. I thought he was exaggerating, right until I met Kaden."

"That didn't change your life. He was right, but you hoped he wasn't."

"What's your point?"

"Unless you want to spend the rest of your life looking for something you're never going to find, you better figure out a way to make peace with what you are."

Shan didn't have a smart comeback. "Fair enough. We can't find that peace here."

Chapter Five

Depot North daybreak Sep 3

"You sure you don't mind me riding along?" Taylor asked, throwing a duffel bag of his gear in the back seat and climbing in to get comfortable. He might nap later.

"We can disagree. You are allowed an opinion." Shannon dropped her stuff in the trunk and walked around to the front of the car, inspecting the tires as she went. Today, she was driving, running shotgun for a caravan heading in from the west. She didn't mind the duty, knowing she'd be snowbound soon. From the outside, to the Council and civilians, it looked like a demotion. She didn't care if that's what people thought, either. It was a pause.

"So I can drive?"

"You can walk to The Vista," she smiled, getting behind the wheel. "Or hop a ride and don't tell me how to drive." They'd be following behind five semis, so forty miles could take a couple of hours. Another caravan vehicle was out in front, with armed guards as well-not Security, not civilians either, but people trained for caravans.

"Are you in Dispatch today?"

"I have a run tomorrow, Dispatch next week. They're considering moving me out to Station One. Most people don't enjoy setting out there for weeks, especially the older officers. They know us children have taken over the city." Dozens of houses had been rebuilt in Anaconda and occupied in recent years. Most of the residents were Security officers and their families. All of them were under forty. "I'm going to transfer to Cody when the weather lets me be brave enough to fly."

"Kerrie is walking all over the place," he changed the conversation to a safer subject. "I think she's going to be climbing by winter. I'm not volunteering for anything out in the snow. I need to be at home, lending a hand. Tara has made it clear."

"I bet she has," Shan said. Her niece was adorable, and very active, at a little over a year old.

"Once we get home, come visit." He settled in to read a bit. A few minutes later, they turned on to the main road.

"Kind of slick out on the pavement," Shan commented.

He grunted a response, feeling them fishtail a bit, immersed in a book, an actual paper copy. They had buildings full of them for posterity.

"Taylor."

"I know, I know, it's supposed to snow."

"Kyle," she snapped. "Black ice."

His gaze shot up to the semi in front of them. "Slow down then."

"Good plan, but we're already on the ice."

"As long as he doesn't hit his brakes," he said as the taillights on the truck lit up, indicating that was exactly what was happening.

"Shit," they both said.

"Black ice in all lanes," she radioed the lead car.

The trailer began a slow-motion swerving to the left, the driver losing control. Shan down-shifted, having no other option. The space between them was rapidly closing. She turned into the slide as the car hit more ice, watching his brake lights flash again.

Then the semi jack-knifed, the trailer swinging back towards the center of the road. "Shit," she repeated, knowing it would be futile to hit the brakes. "Impact." Diving over in the seat, she covered her head with her hands, the car plowing into the trailer's midsection at forty miles an hour.

"Code Three, repeat Code Three, location twelve miles east of Garrison," someone on the radio reported, sounding out-of-breath.

"Car wreck." Lambert was in dispatch with Cassie. She was interested in the job, wanting to train in all the fields. He'd volunteered to take the shift with her. Having a code call right off, he was rethinking that idea.

"Caravan?" Cassie asked. It didn't sound like Security, or at least anyone she had worked with.

"Check the board and see who," he directed, alerting the ambulance crew and a Security team. "This is Station Two, an accident east of Garrison. The roads are wet and icy in spots. Call in for details when you're on the road."

"It's a caravan coming in from Missoula," she confirmed, flipping through the list on the clipboard. High-tech stuff The Vista relied on. "Taylor and Allen are supposed to be running with them this morning."

Something didn't sound right. "Missoula caravan," he got back on the radio. "What's going on out there?"

"The pavement is solid ice. We just lost two trucks and the tail gunner. There are injuries. We need a tow truck, a big one, to pry them apart."

"Which car?"

"The Security team."

"Fuck," Lambert said, not on the air, then calling the emergency crew. "We need responders with extraction equipment, multiple vehicle accident with injuries. Expect icy conditions." He flipped to another channel. "Capt. Allen, Capt. Taylor, call-back Station Two." Silence. He wondered if Wade knew. Team Three had not only been disbanded, they'd developed ways to better keep themselves separated from each other.

He switched channels again. "Cmdr. Duncan, we have a Code Three involving Security."

"Should we alert the hospital?" Cassie asked when there was no immediate answer.

"They'll know when the ambulance goes out and gets a report right from the scene. So will the fire station." He thought about it, then went to a private channel. "Capt. Green, Officer Taylor, this is Lambert. Call me if you can hear me." This time of year, he never knew who was on duty, and who had transferred to another Station, or city, now that they had the Cody base.

"This is Green. I have half a shift left at the hospital. Taylor Two is out at Station Three, getting ready to rotate back in tonight. What's happening?"

"That code call going out to Garrison is Allen and Taylor One, neither responding on their radio. Someone needs to find out where Wade is."

"You're right, and it looks like I'm it. Hope he's at home."

"Keeping 'Conda business to ourselves?" Cassie asked.

"All we can do is try. We don't contact next of kin until we know what's going on. Right now, it could be a fender bender. No need to cause worry until we have to." His worry, that it was no accident and was about to turn into a Security incident.

She nodded, remembering how it had been a few months earlier, when a bunch of them had gone off to Colorado. Lambert wouldn't talk about it, and Team Three, or the people who had been in Team Three, pretended it had never happened.

"Station Two, this is Duncan. Update me when you get a report from the scene."

"What do we do now?" Cassie asked.

"We wait to see who shows up first. Get comfortable."

She smelled something burning first, and tried to move. She couldn't and didn't know why. Then after a bit, she tried again, more awake, and remembered. Ice, then a wreck. Shan knew the amount of paperwork she had to file was astronomical. Duncan was going to call her in to his office and ask her when she learned to drive. If she could get out of the car.

A hollow thunk, someone hitting the side of the car, brought her back closer to consciousness. "What?" she snapped, not being able to get her bearings. It was dark, and everything hurt. Trying to kick her door was a big mistake.

"You alive?" Kyle asked from the back seat.

"Damned if I know," she managed, in pain.

"They're going to get us out in a couple of minutes. Are you hurt?"

"I think my leg is broken, the left one, maybe both of them. Something is pinning me."

"Steering wheel or dash. Don't move around. There's glass everywhere."

"Are we on fire?"

"No, not us. One of the trucks." There was a muffled discussion outside. "Hang on, I think the tow is here," he attempted to reassure her, and himself.

After a few more minutes of talking she couldn't quite understand, there was metallic clanking. Shan assumed they were hooking up chains to the rear axle. The first jolt of movement startled her. It only took her a moment to realize the odd noise, like rain, was someone dumping sand to keep sparks from starting another fire.

"They said they're ready," Kyle told her. "Here we go."

When the vehicles broke apart, the car lurched backwards, bumping into the tow truck. Shan had a few choice words, covered in glass and dirt. The roof of the car was peeled back like an old tin can, and she blinked at the bright sunlight. Kyle sat up, dazed.

A caravan medic leaned over the car, assessing the pair. "Can you tell me your name?"

She glared up at him, disoriented.

"Shan, come on," Kyle said.

"You just told her what her name is," the medic pointed out. He was a poster boy for tall, dark, and handsome, with deep brown eyes, long brunette hair tied back, and a trimmed mustache and goatee.

Shan smiled at him, getting her bearings back.

Kyle made a sound of disgust.

"Oh, dear gawd," she exhaled. "I'm Shannon Summer Allen. I was born on Dec. 2nd, 2037, at the Deer Lodge Memorial Hospital, before they got the power back on and started calling it The Vista. Right now, I'm a Scout captain in Vista Security, but sometimes I'm a lieutenant. It varies from week to week. I have a twin brother who's three minutes younger than me, and annoying as hell. Ask him his name."

"Kyle Taylor, Scout Capt., something else I'm supposed to say."

"The annoying twin," Shan said.

He looked back at Kyle for confirmation. "I see the family resemblance."

"We're fine," Kyle said. A pair of caravan drivers helped Taylor out of the remains of the car and started triage.

"I'll decide that. I'm Lucca, I'm going to check you out, Capt. Allen, and get you on your way to the hospital."

"Shannon."

"We're on duty, Capt. Allen." He took her vitals and moved on, satisfied. "Can you move your feet?"

"Left leg, not so good," she grimaced.

He gave her a thumbs up as she did, moving on to a quick pat-down. She flinched when he got to her left leg. "We're going to get you on a backboard and move you out of the car."

"It's not my spine," she said, for Kyle's benefit.

"No, but it's the easiest way to get you loaded up and on your way. I'm cutting your jeans so I can get an air cast in place," Lucca went on. "Maybe broken, maybe not." Most of the time, his patients were hysterical, uncooperative, or both. It took no time to get her prepped, finishing by throwing a heavy blanket over her. It was snowing. He motioned for the others. "Now it's time for a bit of painkiller," he said, giving her a hypo in the thigh at the same time. "All done."

"Needles don't bother me," Shan told him. Lucca was one of Wade's hidden assets, she decided, feeling the painkiller working. "That's some really nice drugs you got, though."

Four of them hoisted her onto the stretcher, then up and over the remains of the car. She got a glimpse of the wreckage. "I want to see the video footage of this," she called out, glancing over. "You look like shit, Capt. Taylor."

"So do you, Capt. Allen. Let's get going."

"You can't ride in the back with her," Lucca told him. "One per emergency vehicle."

"Neither can you," Kyle said. "She's Security Command, and you gave her morphine. Trade secrets. You get both of us, or you ride up front."

Lucca rubbed an eye, knowing how uptight Security could be, and uncertain if it was an actual issue or the twin being as annoying as she'd claimed. "You got morphine too."

"I'm not in Command."

"Load him up," Lucca decided. "You're both stable, so enjoy the ride."

It was a nightmare, she knew, and there was nothing she could do to stop it. The fear was already there. Shan could hear voices outside, somewhere, arguing and shouting. She moved to the window, recognizing the room as one of the private chambers for Council on the second floor of City Hall. The view west revealed Station Two, burning, and a bonfire in the street out front. People were fighting, baseball bats, 2×4s, anything they could find. Someone was shooting randomly from the rooftop of the old bank.

"Get away from the window," a disembodied voice warned.

There was no one else in the room. Shan turned to look. It was pitch black, and empty, creaking like old buildings do.

Fire in the Station was spreading upwards, glass breaking, smoke whipping in the air like there was a wind. She went back to the scene unfolding, knowing a group of Vistans were about to come out of the bank and confront the Scavengers en masse. Security had re-enacted the scenario with trainees, over the years, showing them how things could go wrong, and how things could go right, in the middle of an attack.

"I said, get away from the window," Rafe growled, striding into the room. He grabbed her by the hair, dragging her back towards the blackness beyond the doorway.

It was like she was in water, moving in slow motion, trying to fight back, to break away. He spun her around, hand on her throat.

A brilliant flash of light from outside drew their attention, and he released his grip on her. The light grew until it blotted out everything else. They both stared, watching as it faded. Shan knew what it was, knew it was the warhead on the Missouri Breaks. Then the people outside began screaming. The windows shattered inwards.

Shannon whipped around, lurching halfway out of the bed, swearing when she knocked her crutches over and banged her foot on the table. The room looked like any compact, neat bedroom, a hand-made bedspread, curtains on the window, pastel yellow walls. A hospital room for non-critical patients and occasional travelers.

A nurse leaned in the door. "Everything all right, Officer Allen?"

"Wonderful, thank you," Shan said to the woman, who was only being polite and doing her job.

She nodded and left.

With her leg aching from hip to toes, Shan regarded the crutches on the floor. She leaned back, contemplating how to retrieve them without calling the nurse or hurting herself. When she opened her eyes again, the crutches were propped against the wall, and Green was sitting in the chair, reading.

"That was weird," she announced. "I didn't hear you come in."

"I'm stealthy," he said, continuing to read.

"But I should have known you were here."

He put the book down. "Nightmares?"

"Yeah, one hell of a one. New one."

"Want to talk about it?"

"Nope. Later"

"Taylor's down the hall, busted arm, a few ribs. The concussion kept him here. The on-duty nurse said you stayed when they told you to go. Did you get a knock on the head, too?" Her dislike of the hospital wasn't a secret.

"New Security class, bivouac. My room at home has four clueless trainees that are due to get dragged out and dumped somewhere in the mountains in a few hours. The station is worse." She fidgeted, not comfortable, not expecting to get that way soon.

"Want something for the pain?"

"What did you have in mind?"

"Happy drugs."

Shan grinned. "You know me so well."

"That I do."

"They gave me something at the crash site. Morphine."

"Over nine hours ago. Don't let them give you more. I doubt they would anyway." Motioning for her to scoot over, he sat on the edge of the bed and produced a small, hand-rolled cigarette. "Until our parents' generation, it was illegal to use cannabis in a lot of places."

"They had a movie about how evil it was, from the 30s, the 1930s, out at Station One last winter. It was so ridiculous, it was funny."

He lit it, inhaled, and passed it to her. Shan did the same. She didn't smoke often, and rarely, for recreation. They started coughing, Green recovering faster.

"Good stuff," he said, taking it for another hit. "Refreshing."

Shan laughed, waving her hand to dissipate the smoke. "We aren't supposed to smoke in the hospital."

"If that nurse comes back and throws me out, come to the station. I've got a room for the week."

"By yourself?"

"I've been working here four days a week, Security three, then off for three. It's easier to keep a room than have someone driving me out to the Ranchlands every day. We could turn up the radio and make some noise of our own."

She hoisted her broken leg up. "Not with this."

"I don't know, we might figure something out," he wagged his eyebrows.

"They rescheduled the flight from Angelfire. Hunter will be here next week."

"Ah, I see. It's been a while."

"Three months."

"Good grief, woman. How do you live like that?" He was aware she'd been celibate.

Before she could answer, there was a rapping on the door. Deirdre, Dr. Allen, dressed in her purple hospital smock, came in. "What are you two up to?"

"Nothing," they both responded, Green standing up and grinning at Shan.

"I can smell whatever you've been smoking."

"Leg aches," she said.

"We have things for that here."

"I'd rather talk gossip with him and smoke a little, instead of having nightmares, because that's what those pills do for me all the time."

Deirdre regarded each of them.

"Jeez, Mom, you're jumping to conclusions."

"Do you think I didn't know what was going on in my own home? I was worried about you and Wade when you joined Security."

Shan grimaced, knowing what was next. "Wade is my best friend.

Talking about him and sex at the same time is just gross. There was nothing to 'worry' about. Mac and I had a relationship for a long time. So have Damon and I."

"I caught you two," Deirdre said, nodding at Green. "If you don't remember, I certainly do."

"I remember," Green volunteered.

Shan looked aghast. "We were sleeping."

"Well, we were asleep by the time she came home early," he offered.

"Damon, shut up. You're not helping."

He suppressed a grin and shut up.

"I'm not blind, Shannon. I didn't want you to get hurt," her mother told her.

"There's no way to avoid it, at some point." She didn't elaborate.

"We're all adults. It doesn't stop me from wanting my child to not know that pain."

"But I'm okay. I'll be okay, he'll be okay," she bobbed her head towards Green. "Mac and I will always be close. Hunter, I may strangle someday, but I think that's a mutual feeling."

Deirdre hugged her, then Green. "I didn't mean to embarrass you."

"Too late." Shan swung her legs over the edge of the bed, Green handing her the crutches. "While I have you both here, I need to talk to you." She hobbled across the room and pushed the door shut. "Before today, plans were in motion to move 'Conda members, in anticipation of everything shutting down for the season. Those plans have changed."

"You're speaking as Capt. Allen," Deirdre said.

"No. We've always kept individual people, our own back-up team, of sorts. Green has been with me since I was put on the road. Sometimes we include civilians. In this case, no one will have a problem."

"You mean me," Deirdre said.

"Green already knows what he's supposed to do if I need help."

"I'm not in Security. They insist I shoot a gun once a year to keep our house open to officers. I can't see what help I'd be."

"Exactly. I need someone Council wouldn't connect to my Security duties. You're perfect."

"What do I do?"

"Nothing, for now. Just be aware, if an emergency were to happen, I might be coming to you for that sort of help."

"You wouldn't, before now?"

"Of course I would. It might not be an emergency others would be aware of. Like Council."

"Or Command," Green added, serious now.

She was quiet for a moment. "Anything either of you need. Does this include anyone else?"

"Hunter more than me," Green said.

"Both of you, for now. Mac and Wade have their own arrangements." Shan shrugged, knowing they had plans within plans that she didn't know about.

"Team Three was disbanded," Deirdre said.

"Technically, yes. In reality, until we get back out in the world, accurate enough."

"Out where?"

"That's the thing. We need someone in the field. Mac is stuck in Cody. We thought he'd be able to get out, but that's not the case. Wade can't. He asked me if I was interested."

"That's why Hunter is coming in," Green said.

"No one suggested I ask him, but I did."

"Out where?" Deirdre asked, understanding. "Where are you going out to?"

"There is no mapped plan. We're just going to go. Mix in with other travelers and see what we can."

"This time of year?"

"Maybe not until spring," Green said. "It depends on how fast her leg heals."

"Eight weeks or more," Deirdre said. "You should know that."

"Wade broke his wrist when he was ten jumping out of a tree house across the street from our original home here," Shan said. "Nine days in a cast."

"It wasn't as bad as we thought, maybe only a sprain." Deirdre let it go, then shook her head. "I've seen it with all three of you that you heal too fast."

"Normal medical things aren't always true for us. Maybe not until spring." Shan repeated. "There are a lot of factors involved. Things I won't discuss, and there's the weather."

"Was this wreck an accident?" Green asked what had been nagging him all day.

"Yes," Shan said. "I blinked, and then I was on black ice. It's not the first time."

"Scouts are rough on cars."

"And Guardians. I have ways to contact people. Even if you don't hear things, don't worry. We'll be as safe out there as we are here."

"Is that supposed to make me feel better?" Deirdre asked.

"The idea is to look around. Be careful, mingle with the locals. Listen. Learn." Shan could blend into a crowd. That was the easiest part. "We'll be fine, like we were when we went out in July."

"I hope so. We'll take at home later." Deirdre excused herself to finish her rounds.

"I've got to find someplace to take it easy for a couple days, in case it burns off like other things do," Shan decided. Their unusual healing abilities were countered by a fever. A broken bone was one of the minor injuries they'd suffered.

"My room at the Station, if all else fails."

"Are you taking me up on that proposition?"

"I've seen you with Hunter, and no way I'd get between you and him, all joking aside. You and I, we just play. You tried to ignore him for months and it didn't work." He leaned close, whispering. "I know what you're doing. This field work wasn't Command's idea. Grab him and run, because this place isn't safe for you, not until all the deep, dark secrets come to light. Maybe not after."

"Can I ask you something personal?"

He regarded her, one eyebrow raised. "Why do you have to ask, if you can ask?"

"Your brother is a shaman, but you know spiritual things, too."

"I know our traditions."

"Do you think we have souls?"

Green was surprised. "You mean The Altered?"

She nodded.

"Of course you do. It doesn't matter what has been done to your DNA, it has no effect on your soul. Those two things aren't connected. You've been listening to the old media feeds again, haven't you?"

"They wanted us destroyed because we were soulless deviants created by science. They didn't even consider us human."

"Don't do that to yourself, Shan. You know better, I know better. If you had no soul, you wouldn't worry about having no soul. Understand?"

She thought about it.

"Mac has the softest heart I've ever known. You'd do anything to help people, and Wade is destroying himself, trying to protect people like the ones who think you aren't human. What does that make them?"

"It doesn't matter."

"Exactly. So many labels, so little compassion. If you had no soul, you wouldn't care. Go ask my brother if you don't think he'll have the same answer." He caught that look, knowing what she was thinking, out of habit rather than some engineered ability. "You worry more about Wade than yourself."

"I talk a mean streak, but I don't think I could do the things he's done."

"You would, if you had to. I was in Manitou. I know what happened. It's never been a matter of choice."

"I hope you're right."

"You know I am."

"Someone has to have his back. I'm the most qualified."

"Someone has to have yours, too."

"Is that you?"

Green didn't offer an answer.

"If they call us out for being Altered, don't let them drag you in. Distance yourself, hell, run away. I won't be offended. I could make it an order."

He snorted.

"You've already started by taking a job here."

"I'd always planned to. The offer was too good to pass."

"Didn't that make you suspicious?"

"Of course."

"Good," she smiled. "Take me out to breakfast, and I'll tell you all about our plans for the winter."

"Nightfall is in half an hour," he pointed out, gathering his coat. "I'll buy you supper and listen, anyway."

"I must have slept less than I thought. Painkillers mess me up."

"If you talk nice to me, I'll drive you out to my place, and you can use it until you're ready to go back to work."

"You, Capt. Green, have a deal."

Chapter Six

The Vista afternoon Oct 17

Wade found it by accident while picking through a pile of dusty pre-war artifacts, in search of something for a birthday present. A little more than a pamphlet, turned around backwards and missed because it looked like part of a larger book. 'SeaTac Metro Technologies Compendium of the Rock Creek Haven Facility'. The title took up two lines on the cover, and he guessed it couldn't be more than forty pages thick. He thumbed through, thoughts not on the party for Shan later. Slipping it inside his jacket without the notice of the library clerk, he decided it was time to pay Cmdr. Perro a visit.

"My mother is still, under the impression Rock Creek was created by the group called Haven, to sneak The Altered away from those who created them," he said, getting straight to his concerns. The office Perro occupied wasn't large or elaborate, but still quite secure. He checked twice a week.

"That's been my impression as well," he said, offering Wade a double shot glass of whiskey. "What have you heard?"

Wade took the whiskey and placed the booklet on his desk. "They missed this when they purged the library. There was twenty years of dust on the stacks, but it was printed after the war, probably right here."

"Do you dig through old media often?" Perro wondered, having a look.

"Shannon, Capt. Allen's birthday is soon, and she collects old books."

"I don't imagine you should give her this one," he said, reading on. It didn't take long for him to skim through. He rubbed his eyes. "What do you plan on doing with this information?"

"Ask your advice on what I should do."

It had been a long time since Team Three asked for advice. "This," he said, handing it back to Wade, "is game changing. This is what you and I and half the people in Security have suspected since there was a Security. It's also a time bomb. We sealed up Rock Creek for a reason. Council wants proof The Altered congregated here. This is the proof. Both good and bad. Even setting aside discretion, they wouldn't have a way to decide whom. Team Three has been discussed and dismissed more than once. Dismissed, because your abilities are not something documented, or expected. They can't pinpoint you or anyone. That's good for us. The bad," he shrugged. "Unfounded fears."

"Unfounded now."

"True."

"What do we do?"

"Get your affairs in order. When or if you confront them, they'll come at you from all sides. They will question your loyalty to Council, to Security, to The Vista, even to your family. This involves your team, and they need the same warning."

"With this, Council will want answers about Colorado. We buried those reports in Command files."

"They might get to them through legal means."

"They're going to exile us," Wade said.

"Is it that bad?" Perro asked, even as he nodded yes.

"We made a point of protecting Mac."

"Command noticed he was conspicuously absent. Almost. Enough that the Council might not harbor any suspicions. Then again, they might. I lean towards not, because they don't seem to be fixated on him. You are another story."

"I understood that, long before I left Command for Council."

"Trying to throw them off."

"It worked, for a few months."

"They were using the position to keep track of you, keep you confined to The Vista, as much as you were using them to glean all that hidden information you've always thought they hid away." Perro indicated the pamphlet. "Then you find this, by accident."

"Was it an accident?" Wade asked.

"If I had this sort of information, I'd just hand it to you."

"Good point," he said. Perro had always been honest with him. "Once I've gotten what I can from Council and conferred with my partners, how should I approach this?"

"There's a Council meeting on the day after tomorrow. Get someone affiliated with Cody to present separation papers. Push it through, and in thirty days you can call a vote. After that happens, do what you need to. Say the things you've held back. Remember who will hear you."

Wade nodded.

"Can you hold on to this for thirty days?"

"Another month is nothing and gives me time to talk with Mac and Shan. The rest is up to Council."

"Let's go for a walk and find Capt. Allen a proper birthday gift."

Wade followed, uncertain what they were doing. They donned parkas and headed across the park, boots crunching in the snow. "I thought your office was safe."

"It is, but if we sit in there too long, word will get around, and then Council will think we've been having secret meetings. So, we're out in public."

"Members of the 'Conda are going to want to go to Cody."

"They're free to go, although they may be dismissed from Vista Security," Perro said.

"They'll be Cody Security. Capt. Lambert will brief them as time permits."

"Remember, you don't have much. That SeaTac Metro Tech built Rock Creek may not be as significant as we think. What do you know about Council striking a deal with Councilor Vance?"

"Right after the bomb on the Missouri Breaks. Until recently, I was trying to piece events together. This little book turns out to be the missing piece. Council struck a deal with him, that if they uncovered any Altered, they'd tell him, and in return, he wouldn't bomb us. The Altered were here, because of Rock Creek, and Vance was aware."

"They may not have had another option."

"No. They couldn't know the bomb was an accident caused by Rafe. He and Vance were watching for us, even then, waiting to see if we developed any abilities they could use."

"So it can't happen again? I mean, the warheads." It was a genuine concern. The Vista had been spared fallout from the detonation because it happened on the other side of the Continental Divide.

"According to Capt. Allen, no, and she knew the situation with Rafe best."

"Good, that's one thing I'm relieved to not consider ever again." They stopped in front of one of the caravan centers, a sorting area for goods brought in from other places. "Get your people organized. Command will back you, but there's only so much we can do. What does Capt. Allen like?"

"Excuse me?"

"Does she like jewelry, clothes, art? Her birthday party is tomorrow, and you didn't find a book."

"I didn't," Wade agreed. "She likes eclectic things. I never know what will catch her eye."

"Then find her something eye-catching."

"You're aware our relationship isn't what most people perceive."

"You see each other as siblings," Perro stated. "Obvious to those of us that are familiar. Books are plentiful, and I imagine ninety percent of the gifts you've ever given her. Surprise her with something different, something unique."

"Thank you, sir."

"I know you have plans in place. When it breaks to Council, expect chaos. Command can cover anyone who didn't go to Colorado even if they are 'Conda members. The rest of you knew the chances you were taking when you started this."

"We did. We'll be ready."

"They're arguing about jurisdiction, and the meeting hasn't been called to order yet," Taylor said, having a select audience in the comm center at Station Two. His brother was sitting next to him, in the room with Dallas, Hunter, Cassie Elliott, and Quinlen. The joint Command and Council meeting was happening a few buildings away and wasn't open to the public.

"How can you tell?" Cassie asked.

Lucca Riley let himself in, and she scooted over a chair. "Sorry," he whispered. "On-call staff meeting ran overtime. So many meetings, so little purpose."

"We have a purpose. Capt. Allen is wearing an open mic," Taylor said, tapping his ear. "Also, she is the only one attending aware of this." He had people waiting for reports, Green out at the Ranchlands on his day off and Ballentyne in Cody. Others, too. This would affect them all.

"Jurisdiction of what?" Dallas asked.

"Rock Creek. Wade came in a few minutes ago, said Council was trying to get ahead of us, and stormed off to the meeting."

"What's Rock Creek?" Lucca asked, being an outsider.

"A Security cache."

"A cache. Why would they want to annex a cache, and why is Wade pissed?"

They all looked at each other. "Quinlen," Taylor said. "Can you get on the other radio and ask Ballentyne to ask Mac that question? This is more than Council trying to push Command." He was annoyed at not thinking of the question himself. Too many issues at hand.

"Got it," he said, going to the smaller station set off in a corner. The room was set up with three separate radios, but more than one was seldom in use.

"I wish we could watch," Chris said.

"No, you don't," Quinlen said. "It can get ugly. You'd understand better how wars got started if you saw how neighbors and friends act towards each other."

"Roll call, recognizing who is there and who's absent. Both have quorums. That's unusual, too. Chairperson Haines is speaking first," Taylor told them.

The radio blared, signaling a call from Security, and Taylor went to a headset, motioning for his brother to take the call on the earpiece he'd been listening on.

"Of course there's a call," Quinlen said.

"Code Two, Team Eleven, halfway to Station One. Team One," Chris waved at Dallas and Hunter. "You're up."

"Shit," Hunter drawled as he and his partner grabbed their gear. "Keep us informed, if it's something important."

Taylor nodded, waving an acknowledgment. "They're still nitpicking semantics of the laws, but they're calling to order now. Maybe. If everyone would shut up for a minute."

Long intervals of discussion over other subjects were first on the agenda. One being the annual Sweeps, which had been discontinued because of several diplomatic delegations heading out. Estes Park was not one of those places. Another brief about the separation of Station One at Anaconda, official as of five months earlier. Taylor recited back to them, understanding, but knowing their impatience wouldn't accomplish a thing. These meetings often stretched on for hours. Quinlen wandered out with a headset, waiting for an answer from Cody, returning with a carafe of hot coffee and passing it around.

"Haines recognized Lambert," Taylor announced. "He's telling them he has separation papers for Cody, accepted by Command at their last meeting." They all waited for a response from the Council. The Anaconda separation had gone through without issues. This was different. This could be seen as open rebellion rather than natural expansion.

"They accepted the papers," he said. "Wade can call a vote at the next meeting. Relay that to Green and Ballentyne." He paused. "Now they're arguing about Rock Creek and if it's in the legal definition of The Vista," Taylor said. "Ten-mile rule is the problem."

"It's fifteen and a half miles, by maintained roads." Quinlen knew, since he'd driven it hundreds of times. "That's the mileage that counts."

"One hundred percent true," Chris agreed. He'd taken up a study of Vista laws. There was a lot of empty time on long winter shifts to occupy.

"Yes," Taylor said, trying not to fidget. "Council is aware." A pause. "I don't recognize the voice, but a Council member is calling for a public vote to annex Rock Creek to the city."

"From Cody," Quinlen interrupted. "Cmdr. MacKenzie says at this time he cannot disclose any information about Rock Creek."

"Fuck," Lucca added his color commentary.

"Fuck, indeed," Taylor agreed. "That means Rock Creek is not just a cache. Cmdr. Perro said sure, go ahead with an annexation, as long as they include full disclosure about the facility. Lots of arguing now."

"Disturbing stuff," Cassie said. "Now I remember why I stay away from these things."

"I can't tell who is saying what. I think Shan got up and moved. Someone is asking for a vote, to see if they're going to ask for a public vote."

"Perro will do it, and he'll tell people about Rock Creek," Quinlen said. "My question, what is it, and will anyone care?"

"Council is betting they will. Good for them, bad for Security." Taylor had never been part of conversations about the place. He didn't have a clue either.

"Legally, Security has full control over the facility, inside The Vista or not," Chris said.

"Tell the Council."

"Send me over."

"Well?" Cassie asked after a few more tedious minutes.

"They're voting on a referendum to call a public vote. A simple majority is what they need." It was nerve-wracking listening in. "Wade voted against it, and so did his stepfather. I don't recognize the other voices. They're too far away." Then, "It's a tie."

"How Security-friendly is Haines?" Lucca asked.

"Maj. Ballentyne is his nephew, so he leans towards Security a lot," Quinlen said. "As long as he thinks he has a good reason to."

"He voted against the resolution," Taylor exhaled. "Council is throwing a lot of accusations, but the vote has been tabled." He glanced around the room, a look of growing alarm on his face. "They want the records Command sealed, the ones about Manitou." Even if they weren't the truth, there were complications, to make it believable.

"They can't have them," Cassie said.

"They can demand to review even sealed files, if they get the consensus it's for the safety of The Vista," Quinlen said. "It means another vote, and this differs from an annexation." They all stared at Taylor as he continued to listen.

"Wade refused to vote because of a conflict of interests. Council got the majority." Taylor spun his chair. "They want to interview the senior officers involved. Meaning they're going after Team Three."

"That, they can't do," Quinlen said. "Not without Command approval."

"True, and they might get it," he said. "Stranger things have happened." Then he went on the air, "Team One, status update."

"Five minutes out," Hunter replied.

"Make it half time." To the room, "The team won't sit around and wait for an inquest."

"What, then?" Lucca asked. "Run?"

"Yes, both, but not together. Don't ask." He switched channels. "Green, we need you flight-ready now. Council is going after the Colorado team." He wouldn't say Team Three, in case anyone else was monitoring the channel.

"On the way."

Taylor switched channels again, listening. "Wade just walked out of the meeting and Allen was right behind him. Heads up, they aren't going to take this lightly." He spoke to the room, and to concerned relatives, listening on their own radio frequency.

"You were in Manitou," Quinlen reminded him, as if he needed to.

"Team Three will be the focus until they're not. Right now, we need to worry about their reactions."

"Flight-ready?" Lucca repeated. "To Cody?"

"Yes. Shan for certain. Hunter will go with her."

"Wade?"

"He'll be gone and maybe we'll have a clue where."

"Capt. Allen will," Lucca guessed. "I'm with the caravans. Clear of this."

Taylor nodded, wondering how the medic was involved with the teams.

"What about Green?" Quinlen asked.

"They can't touch him. He is a citizen of the Ranchlands, not The Vista, and they're separate entities. Council won't even try," Taylor said. "I suggest anyone with affiliations to the 'Conda consider their future here. I'm calling Cody," he went on. "Station Two, private channel." After a few moments, he changed radios. "I need to speak with Maj. Ballentyne."

"Contacting him now," whoever was on the other end answered.

"Lambert wasn't there," Cassie said, concern growing.

"He'll go to Cody," Taylor told her. "On the same flight as Shan, if he has good sense. It's one of their arrangements. I don't know if it's permanent."

"Can I go?"

"Now? I'd wait until the smoke from this clears, then transfer out."

"If he goes today, I want to go today."

Taylor shook his head. There was no time to argue, and it might as well be a full flight. "You better get home and pack. There's a forty-five-pound weight limit, but you can have more shipped over later."

She jumped up, heading out of the comm room, passing Team One as they returned.

The call from Cody came in. "What's happening, Station Two?" Ballentyne asked.

"Too much to put on the air. You're going to have company in a few hours. They can tell you all about what I can't."

"Who are we getting?"

"Capt. Allen," Taylor said, looking at Hunter, who nodded affirmative. "Hunter, Lambert, Cassie Elliott."

"Quinlen?" Ballentyne asked, knowing who was being targeted. Another nod.

"Yes," Taylor said. "I'm holding on here."

"Got it. I'll get with Cmdr. McKenzie. Someone from the airfield will contact them once they're moving."

"We're out."

"Do you need to get home?" Chris asked his brother.

"Yeah, I do," Kyle decided, having had a few minutes to think about it. "They won't try to stop us, not today. It's easier that way. They won't have to explain to the public, to civilians, what happened. It will be a series of transfers to Cody, and then we're out of their jurisdiction. I'm not jumping unless I have to." He had his family to consider.

"Is this going to affect the Cody separation?"

"No. Team Three said this is what the Council wants. After the debacle today, I'd say they were right."

"You're welcome to stay in Cody," Mac spoke to Hunter as they stood on the veranda, away from the growing crowd. "Or head to Angelfire when the weather clears. Your choice."

Pod One was well lit, warm, furnished, and hosting the unexpected planeload of Vistans. Green would make the return trip at dawn. The rest were new residents of Cody. Because of the limited space, it was possible they'd be sleeping in the main floor lobby for a few nights. Their few belongings were piled in a corner while they chatted with other officers. Each of them had a different story about what had happened.

"Do you know what they're going to do?" Hunter asked. Shan, out of earshot in the lobby, laughed about something Lambert said. Cassie was laughing, too. Relieved to see them smiling, he was still worried. "I mean Team Three."

"Since the moment we killed Rafe, we haven't made new plans. All this conflict with the Council was considered before we were aware of Estes Park, and then was everything that came after. So the answer is no, I don't know what Wade is doing, and I can only make an educated guess at what Shan's intent is. My suggestion, ask her."

"She wants to go to Angelfire. I'd be content to stay there for the season."

"I guarantee you, things are in motion. Take her to Angelfire. Stay there. Listen to her, but be aware this isn't finished. It might be Command leading her towards the next step out of Montana, it might be Wade, it might be someone or a collective we aren't considering. It's not out of the question to think she's following her own initiative, either."

"If I ask you something in confidence," Hunter said, "I need an honest answer, even if it's not what you think I want to hear."

"You can ask, and if I can't answer, I'll tell you why."

"Can I protect her?"

Mac glanced past him to her. It was a question he'd contemplated, too. "She doesn't need or want someone to protect her. You are as capable as anyone to go out into the world with her."

"I get it," Hunter said. "We're all guessing. She steps up to bat for Wade and the rest of us watch to see what happens."

"That is an accurate statement. I have to go welcome everyone, then get on the radio and talk about the situation back home. Don't expect everyone to stay here. We've wanted to go, and when the weather allows an opportunity, I know of at least two caravan groups heading out."

"Cody's purpose is to protect The Vista, or it was. Has that changed?"

"Not at all. They've been content, and basically against progress or change. It's fear of what they might find out here. You can't blame them. Hell, you're old enough to remember the war. They're right, to a point. The war never ended for a lot of them, and the same will hold true for a good portion of people we meet. We can't let it stifle us."

"We won't," Hunter said.

"Come on and listen, you're as deep in this as the rest of us." Mac walked into the lobby, and the crowd stopped and waited to hear what he had to say. "While you were in transit here, the Council continued their meeting, or called a new one, depending on your perspective."

"Did they have Security issue warrants for us?" Shan got right to the point.

"They did not. However, they have demanded the files from Manitou. Command will surrender them to avoid civilian involvement. We considered this when we wrote the reports. Council has as much to hide, and there will be concessions from both sides."

"So there's nothing to worry about?" Lambert asked.

"The only people now who might have issues are Wade and Capt. Allen." The irony didn't escape Mac. He'd been the one to fire anti-tank missiles into the bunker, killing Rafe and an unknown number of his people. Vance's people. None of that information existed on paper. A significant percentage of the reports were fabricated.

"Wade's in the wind," Green verified.

"Maybe they'll send someone to arrest me," Shan scoffed. "I wonder who."

"Don't joke about it," Green told her, somber.

"What would you do if they did?" Mac asked.

"Be like Wade, and be gone."

"We can get a flight to Angelfire," Hunter said. "Will we have the time?"

"They won't come after her," Mac said. "Expect sanctions. Expect at least temporary exile until they sort through what they have. We knew this could happen. In a month, Cody will legally be free of The Vista. This isn't how we wanted things to progress, but the Council steered it so there was no other choice. Vance will react to all this."

"What sort of response?" Taylor asked.

"We don't have enough information to predict his actions."

"What about the Sixth?" Lambert chimed in. "The factions we've contacted."

"Damned good question," Mac said. "How would you like to go find out?"

Lambert laughed. Then he realized Mac wasn't joking around. "Damn."

"I'll take that as a 'yes'."

He stared out at the expanse of white and cold. The land he'd always known; familiar, comfortable. A thousand miles south, beyond Vance's stronghold, called Skyline, somewhere in central Colorado. A rebuilt city, not self-sufficient, but on a trade route. Well-defended, hidden like The Vista, on the edge of the Great Plains, and on the edge of the Rocky Mountains. He had the opportunity to be safe there, despite being in his enemy's territory.

Wade's other choice was the complete unknown, perhaps a chance encounter with Nomads who might be telling the truth, or spinning tall tales for whatever motives they believed. Cities along the trade corridors, a vast array of settlements and people who didn't know him, and might never realize he was different. There were those places no one could get to. Residual effects of the war made it impossible, and he harbored no desire to challenge the specter of radiation.

In the end, the unknown won.

Chapter Seven

Nebraska mid morning Feb 8 2059

"It might be five miles, or fifty miles," Mitch Elliott addressed their current situation, peering out at the landscape with binoculars. "Everything is flat and white." Accurate, as the storm overnight had dropped a few inches of snow.

Beside him, Kyle Taylor, looking through his own set of glasses, nodded. "Yeah." They'd camped at the bottom of one of the low rolling hills, in a stand of trees not far off the interstate. "We're close to mile marker 165, if that's any help."

"As much as you'd expect," Chris Taylor told them. "But I know where we are. It's not fifty miles."

"Did you memorize Nebraska?"

"More importantly, where is North Platte?" Mitch asked the important question. "Or are we doomed to freeze to death out here in the Great White Nothing?"

"I thought Canada was the Great White Nothing," Lambert said, having to add his opinion.

"North," Chris corrected. "Canada is the Great White North." They all turned to look at him, and he shrugged. "Well, it is."

Cassie Elliott remained quiet, still uncertain how to deal with Security officers, or at least those who had taken off in the dead of winter to parts unknown, for reasons no one was talking about. She had her own ideas about why.

Clearing his throat, Chris said, "Ten or eleven miles. That's what maps are for."

"We don't bring maps," Lambert said. "For good reason. Four thousand and a few."

"We're expected in North Platte." Kyle wasn't in charge, and he didn't care to be. He kept them aware of other plans. It had always been his purpose.

"We're meeting Wade, or the Sixth, or who knows who," Lambert said. "Why Nebraska is the real question. Nebraska."

"We're meeting members of the Sixth, representing Black Hills. That's Dakota, South Dakota. Nebraska because it's difficult to get here this time of year. The weather might deter people we'd consider the unfriendly sort. The people who live here consider this neutral ground. Uncontaminated. Not bordering Texas." Kyle recited what Shannon had told him.

Their trek was simpler now that Vista Council and Vista Command were far behind them. Thirty-one days after Team Three scattered, Command denied Council's request for them to be ordered home. There was no actual recourse for the Council. Cody was granted separation without further discussion, and Command went about its usual business. Council went silent about all things involving Security. Few people took notice. The quiet wouldn't last.

"Kansas doesn't border Texas, either." Chris offered his geographical knowledge again.

"Not on those old maps you memorized. It has since the war," Kyle said. "While we get packed and get moving, I have a few things to go over with everyone. Things Capt. Allen expected we might find useful."

"Oh, great," Chris said.

"It won't hurt much," he promised. "First, the Sixth isn't some fancy name for one of the various clans. The name started out as a designation for a particular group of experiments."

"The Altered," Lambert said for clarity.

"Gen En?" Mitch asked.

"Yes," Kyle said. "It wasn't a slur." He packed his gear with care. Taking off on their own in the dead of winter had been complicated. They understood the risks. This might not be nuclear winter, but the weather was harsher than before the bombs detonated and the cities fell dark.

"And now?" Cassie asked.

"Maybe. Depends on who you ask. The Sixth are different, even from other Altered. I can't go into details I don't know. All I can say is that they were more complex, uncontrollable, and unpredictable. We need to have a set plan for dealing with them."

"Is Shan a Sixth?" Chris asked.

"I don't think anyone has asked her, and I'm not going to. It's a personal thing."

"The Sixth and what we call the fourteenth parallel each other," Lambert said. "It's as good as any guess we make, with the information we have."

"North Platte is on the trade routes, so there will be people here from different places. Places we know nothing about. We are from Cody. If anyone asks about Montana, the Sixth, the Altered, our wandering team, or The Vista, you don't understand what they're talking about. Montana is barren, and The Vista doesn't exist. Keep in mind that just because someone acts nice to you doesn't mean they're your friend. Don't talk too much; don't tell them anything. Be careful about making up too many lies, because you have to remember them later."

"Don't trust anyone you didn't come out of Montana with," Lambert said. The same mantra Wade had recited when he went after Rafe a year and a half ago.

"Good advice," Kyle concurred. "Don't go off alone for any reason. Keep together as a group as much as we can. We're the newcomers, and we're here to establish trade for Cody."

"Which is also true," Lambert added, "although a lower priority for now." He pulled himself astride his horse and ushered them on. "Let's go see what's ten or eleven miles up the interstate."

They got onto the interstate, heading east, the snow crunching beneath hooves, five riders, eleven horses. It was cold. It was going to stay cold. If things worked out well for them here, the plan was to camp over until spring. If not, home was a long way back.

Shortly, Kyle stopped, signaling for them to wait. "A big road sign up ahead," he told Lambert, everyone closing ranks to listen.

"We are on a road," Lambert said

"Hold on," Mitch offered, standing in the stirrups, binoculars ready.

"It says 'Welcome to North Platte'," Kyle said. "That's the Platte River Center. No way it stayed standing for the past twenty years."

"That's not all," Mitch said. "It looks like someone painted over it."

"And?" Cassie asked.

He sat down. "I believe it reads 'Here be dragons', with a skull and crossbones added for effect."

"What sort of effect?" Cassie asked.

"To confuse or frighten travelers," Kyle said.

"Do you think it's Kaden?" Lambert asked.

"Whoever is in charge. I don't think it's his clan. It's meant to keep out troublemakers."

"So, it is meant for us?"

"Yeah, there's a good chance," Kyle figured. "Let's go find out."

"Can you imagine if we just let people ride into The Vista whenever they wanted?" Kyle said, taking in the sights.

The outlying areas of the city, residential from appearances, were in various stages of being dismantled, rather than repaired. Neatly stacked piles of lumber, pallets of red bricks, furniture that looked new rather than salvaged, and other construction materials lined cleared streets. People working stopped to watch them pass, making no effort to engage. A few waved.

Farther east and north, following signs along the road, they found activity. A lot of activity. Bars, shops, a casino, and several hotels lined an extensive park. Many of the shops were temporary structures, tents and big trucks, for easier mobility. From the looks of it, most travelers were in for the season, camps along the river appearing more permanent than the shops.

"Neutral ground," Lambert spoke up. "I don't think that means there are no rules."

"Maybe it means the opposite of no rules. If I were to make a guess, I'd think the rules, the laws here, are harsh and unforgiving," Kyle said.

"He's right," Mitch agreed. "We had people ride right to the depots. Before any of us were old enough to care about it, people used to show up in The Vista at random."

"I bet that caused chaos," Cassie said.

"Not as much as you'd imagine," Kyle told her. "They expanded Security to include Scouts when they figured out the Nomads congregated in the gateway cities for winter. Eleven or twelve years ago. It's worked, for the most part. Some things can't be anticipated."

"Tell that to Team Three." Lambert meant it, knowing they weren't the only group of Vistans sent out and about, and that Team Three had organized it all. "This looks like the Welcome Committee." A group of several people, male and female, stood off to the side of the road, waiting. They were bundled up in heavy, well-kept, clean clothes. Armed too, with weapons casually hanging from two of the men's shoulders. "Everyone, stay alert. We're here to make friends and influence people, not start wars."

"Where have I heard that before?" Kyle murmured.

"Wade, every time he goes out," Chris said.

"That's what I get for telling you Security secrets."

"Pay attention," Cassie interrupted them as the villagers approached. "Let's not be Wade today." Lambert pointed and motioned for her to join him. She dismounted and followed.

"Welcome to the Platte River Center," one woman greeted, holding her hands out, palms up, at waist level. Older, with white hair, mahogany skin, and sparkling dark eyes, her voice carried a faint, unfamiliar accent. She was dressed in a pale gray fur parka and heavy pants, white boots, and a strategically worn semi-auto handgun of some sort on her hip. "I am DeTessa Jardin, Elder. All are invited to stay and enjoy our city. The travelers and traders are sparse this time of year, but there are many who stay during the winter." She smiled. "Of course, their prices will be higher, since there is less competition. Most are reasonable; a few are old codgers you might barter with if you catch them in the right mood, or have a good bottle of spirits to share." She indicated the armed men with her. "Our Peacekeepers can answer questions you have about our laws, our city, and our citizens."

"I'm Lambert, this is Cassie, and we're looking for a place to camp for a few weeks, while we wait for friends to join us and the weather to be better."

She nodded. "I'm certain we can accommodate you. May I ask where you've traveled from? This is our off-season."

"We started out from Cody right after the first of the year."

"Cody is a new settlement," DeTessa stated rather than asked. "Where did your people come from before?"

"The north is dotted with tiny villages and scattered camps. A handful of us set up Cody as a gathering point, as a hub of sorts," he explained. "We hope to establish trade." Embellishments of the truth, but only a little. He could live with that.

"Trading is a valuable endeavor. Humans need to learn to build one another up, not break one another down, not to destroy. Do you think we've learned that lesson?" she asked Cassie.

"I don't know. I hope so." Cassie mulled it over. "What do you think?"

DeTessa patted her handgun. "I think humans are intrinsically violent, warmongering creatures. I also think they have an unlimited capacity to learn. It remains to be seen how long it takes. Even then, there will always be those who refuse to evolve, and force the hand of those who try."

"What can we do?"

"We keep trying." She motioned to the Peacekeepers. "They'll show you the way to the visitors' area and be your escorts for a few days while you become acclimated to the city. There are several empty buildings open. Find one you can use, and we'll discuss the terms of your stay over supper at my lodge at dark. All are invited. There will be other Elders joining us as well. We like to know who is staying in our city."

"We'd be honored," Cassie accepted the invitation.

"Very good."

"Did it strike you that we might have found a matriarchy?" Lambert asked as they rejoined their friends.

"Because a woman spoke for them? No." She was as straightforward as her brother. Mitch had learned it from her. "Who would speak for us if Team Three were here?"

"Me, more than likely. That's how it's always been. They observe first."

"Maybe that's exactly what we saw with DeTessa and her crew."

"Maybe," he agreed. "I still have a good idea about this place."

"Ask her," Cassie said.

"Would that be a good idea?" Kyle asked.

"Honesty is the best thing we can do here."

"Like lying about where we're from?" Lambert added.

"It's not so much a lie as being careful," she pointed out. The five of them led their horses through the wide streets, where curious children stopped playing in the snow to watch them pass. "She'd understand that."

"When they find out this place is here, it's going to be a race to see who can get here first," Chris said. "Shan or Wade. We can't drag Mac out of Cody."

"We don't want Mac out of Cody," Kyle said.

"What makes you think they haven't been here?" Cassie asked.

"Nothing at all," Chris said. "They get around more than we do."

Lambert held back, motioning for Kyle to join him. "Do you believe everything the team tells you?"

"Are you trying to start a fight with me today?" Kyle came right back.

"Not at all. Team Three put me in charge of this expedition. You should've stayed home if you had a problem." They were in no position for conflict among themselves, and Lambert wouldn't put up with it. The rest of the team waited out of earshot.

"I'm here because Wade wants me here. I sure as hell would rather be home in The Vista, watching my daughter learn to walk and learn to talk. This is more important. Who are we protecting? It's not Team Three, not now. It's our families."

"Agreed. There are three viewpoints besides our own to consider. They don't always agree with each other, and they don't expect we will either. You and I don't know the same things; you were in Manitou. None of us were. Your perspective is important." Lambert could see he was slowing their progress. Who had given Taylor the order was a mystery, and it wouldn't accomplish much that he could see. "We don't know who else is out here."

"So why do we want Mac out of Cody?" Kyle wasn't conceding. Lambert was right, at least about the part where none of them knew what other teams might do, or if they were the only ones.

"Mac is the cornerstone, the foundation of the team. You might not like it, but it's true. He's the one they've kept hidden, and we'll make certain he stays that way. Any of them would be fine out here alone. Get all three of them together, and you're going to see amazing things."

"I was Wade's second for years," Kyle said.

"Yes, you were, back when they were confined to The Vista. Now it's different; out here, they're different. We both were at Divide during the Blackout. It's gone far beyond that, even. The destruction wasn't caused by them; it was aimed at them. They never wanted this. They never had a choice."

"It's why Wade stays away."

"Part of the reason," Lambert admitted. "None of them believe they can hide what they are. They may have stopped trying, and it could attract the less than scrupulous Altereds."

"Like Rafe?"

"Yes. So we keep quiet and do what we're supposed to."

Kyle got quiet, knowing the truth about how that had ended. It scared him that Shannon would go along with Wade's plans, even to that extreme. They had blown the side out of a mountain to kill Rafe. He hadn't gone alone. An unknown number of Nomads and two Vista Security officers had died in the battle. Kyle had been sitting fourteen miles away, waiting for word, or no word.

The conversation was over as the Peacekeepers came by, showing them a street along the lakefront. Some buildings were like warehouses, others were smaller stores, and all looked well maintained. Lambert peered at a couple, picking a smaller one towards the center of the street. Their escorts radioed in and went about the business of appearing bored.

Cassie ventured in first, looking around at their new home. "This has potential," she declared, claiming a tiny side room as her own by dropping her backpack there.

"I suggest we all clean up and get ready for dinner. It's a couple of hours before dark, so a walk around the park might be in order. Volunteers?" Lambert got back to business, setting up a perimeter and checking the area.

No one volunteered.

"Taylor and Taylor, go check out the neighborhood. I'm going to ask the guards a few questions about protocol." He regarded the Elliott siblings. "I suppose you two can figure out what facilities we have here. Everyone meet back here in an hour." He hung back as Mitch motioned for a private word.

"If we're unaware of what the other Cody officers are doing, how are we supposed to meet up?"

"There was no set timeframe. We're here until Mac sends us new orders."

"What if we're the first Vistans here," Cassie asked, correcting herself, "from Cody? What if we're the first group in from Cody?"

"Don't worry too much about it. The Vista isn't marked on any map, so saying it doesn't mean a thing," Lambert told her. She wasn't Security, she wasn't a civilian. He hadn't worried about that when she asked to join one of the teams heading out. "If we're here first, we make the most of it. Take mental notes of everything. Sooner or later, someone from Team Three will show up and want the details. That's why we're here."

"How long do you think we'll have to wait?"

"Patience isn't one of their strong points," Lambert said, getting a snort from Mitch.

"Then why are we wasting time out here, mapping roads?" she asked.

"The trade routes hold civilization together. They have throughout history, and right here, right now, is no different. It's time we stepped back into civilization."

"Is that the new motto of The 'Conda?" Mitch asked.

"It's one of several motivations." Lambert answered. He'd passed off command of The 'Conda to Ballentyne to take command of this group. "Until we get new orders, or get recalled home, this is our lives."

"Yeah, great," Cassie nodded. "I remember what happened last time people got recalled."

"We're here on orders. Don't piss off Command, don't get fired."

"I'm not in Security."

"This is a Security-based expedition."

"Don't piss off Command," she repeated.

"Don't make new best friends with them, either. They'll put you in charge of something or other, and you'll find yourself in the middle of Nebraska in February," Lambert said.

She wasn't certain if he was being sarcastic or not.

It was a good day. The sun was shining; there were bacon and eggs cooking. The locals were gathering as they did every day, weather permitting. Even when they were snowbound, a handful would find their way up the road, on snowshoes or skis.

Hunter turned the faded wooden chair backwards and took a seat next to Shannon. She was sitting in her chair the standard way, reading a handwritten menu. He'd seen to stabling the horses while she found a place to sit. The sum of their gear was stuffed in three large duffel bags lying at their feet.

The building was rather large, maybe an old strip mall or shopping center, and stacked ceiling-high with every imaginable thing that had been salvaged over the years. Boxes were neat, although most went unlabeled. The cafe could hold about twenty people. On a good day, the way station was packed.

Today was a slow day.

"What did you order, and how are we paying for it?" he inquired. In the few weeks they'd been out on their own, they hadn't had a problem finding a place to stay. When the area was inhabited, rent involved animal husbandry of some sort. He wasn't fond of mucking out stalls and was glad she carried a variety of small items many people along the road had a use for. Books were popular. So were shiny jewelry trinkets. Shan packed a supply of both.

"The breakfast special, and I traded a couple of paperbacks and a fifty-year-old Road Atlas of North America."

"Are we moving on, or staying a few?"

Shan wrinkled her nose, thinking about it. "I don't know yet. Let's see how breakfast goes."

She looked cute, sitting there in her winter camos, hair tied up in a messy bun, armed to the teeth, and sipping tea from a dainty china cup covered in red roses. Hunter suppressed a laugh, but ended up grinning. He'd never tell her she looked 'cute'.

"What?" she asked, a bit self-consciously. He made her crazy on occasion. Usually the good kind of crazy, sometimes not so much.

"You," he gestured. "An H&K long rifle in one hand, a teacup in the other." She wasn't holding a rifle, but it was slung over the back of her chair, as casually as it could be. Almost everyone in the building was armed.

Life outside The Vista was new to them. More specifically, life beyond Team Three. She'd been out in the world, albeit briefly, avoiding humans along the way. This was different, and it didn't bother her much that she wasn't with her team. It had taken some getting used to.

"I'm not leaving weapons in a motel room. Too difficult to replace." She smiled back and took a sip of tea.

"I figure once we make our way to North Platte, we can head west when the weather clears, and see what we can see along this route. Cody or Angelfire, your choice."

"I kind of like not planning things," she confessed.

"You made me promise we'd get back to The Vista this year. I'm just holding up my end."

"We'll get back, but the year is new."

A tall man in blue jeans, a long coat, head topped with a bright orange toque, brought out dishes of steaming hot breakfast. Scrambled eggs, bacon, green beans, and hash browns. Plus a carafe of tea.

"Excuse me," Hunter said, leaning back out of the way. "How far is it to North Platte?"

"The Platte River Center is thirty-five or forty miles. This is North Prairie Center. Keep heading south until you cross the I-80. Turn east."

"Thank you," Shan said.

"Are you with the expeditions? It seems early for it, but you never know."

"We're doing some surveying for the Angelfire Assembly," he name-dropped. Many of the smaller places got supplies from there a couple of times a year. "I'm Hunter." He reserved the right not to reveal his real name.

The tall man nodded. "If you need anything else, speak up. I'm Harvey. Did you get a room at the motel yet?"

"I stopped over, and they said they'd save one." He surveyed the meal as their host returned to the kitchen. "All this for a couple of books."

"Not going to laugh at me for stopping at libraries now, are you?" she asked, taste-testing the eggs. Well seasoned with salt, bell pepper, and onion.

"There are only so many books you can haul on one horse. We need a few other supplies."

"You've seen my room. You can never have too many books or bookshelves full of them." They ate, taking in the scenery. People going about their business. From what they'd seen, there were a couple hundred in the area.

"So, what do you think of the flatlands?" Hunter made conversation as they finished their tea. He didn't like it when she was too quiet.

"I prefer the mountains. Where you're from, are there mountains?" She wouldn't say 'Alabama', because it didn't exist now, and because someone might put together who he was.

Hunter chuckled. "Have you ever heard of the Appalachian Mountains?"

"I have," she said. "I just didn't know they went that far south. Geography is not my strong point."

"They do. Not like what we're used to, but mountains. I have vague memories of that place."

She nodded, knowing he felt uncomfortable discussing anything about his life before.

"Ready to go have a look at the room and get our gear unpacked?" He carried two bags, nodding to the proprietor as they departed.

"Sure. I'd like to come look through the goods here later and maybe walk around. See the sights." She liked to get a feel for a place, and her Gen En abilities might help. Sometimes they did, sometimes they didn't. At the least, she'd decide if they could stay, or if they should get the hell out of town.

"It's a date. We can sightsee, have supper late, and figure out when to get on the road again."

"Perfect."

He stopped, regarding her. "How long have we known each other? Specifically?"

"Specifically, twenty-two months and four days. We met in the middle of the night on the road west of Depot North. Because you didn't know how to drive worth a damn on a little bit of ice." Shan stopped beside him, curious now. "Why?"

"In those twenty-two months..."

"And four days," she added.

"Have I ever acted or reacted in a way that indicated I was stupid?"

"You have not."

"When are you going to tell me why we're out here?"

"We're out here because your father let us wander away in the middle of winter, to do what we're doing. Sightseeing." He wasn't stupid, and she wouldn't tell him a half-truth. "That, and I'm a Command officer."

"I've heard the rumor once or twice."

They continued on towards the motel. In dire need of a fresh coat of paint, the rooms were clean, and the roof didn't leak. The attendant had said so. Seeing that it was the only one within walking distance, and with the horses already boarded for the night, it would do. Besides, it didn't look like rain.

"Do you remember the conversation we had with Kaden in The Vista after Command got hold of us?" she went on.

"Yes."

"You remember mention of certain affiliations concerning our allies, and people we'd rather not be associated with." She always spoke in public as if someone might be listening.

"I remember why we don't go to Texas."

She looked around. A group of people were gathering outside the way station, playing cards and watching the road. Out of earshot. "Skoltech created a specific line of Altereds. All the big biomedical groups did. SeaTac included. Apparently, some Altereds can be identified from their abilities, as to who engineered them."

"Talking about humans like they were a science project still pisses me off," he said. He brushed it away, his anger pointless. It had all started long before he was born. "My question. Do you know which corporation messed with your genetics?"

She looked troubled for a moment. No one had ever asked. Wade and Mac knew; a few others assumed. "I do."

"Want to share?"

"I'm not certain it's relevant to why we're here."

"Why are you afraid to tell me?"

"Because of that, because of who altered me."

Hunter looked beyond her facade; he always had. It bothered her more than she'd admit. "I don't care."

"Most of the corporations were civilian, but some attached to governments, and they were military. Some went as far as sharing information. Several facilities could be involved."

"And?"

"The biotech that edited my genetics was affiliated with NORAD." The North American Aerospace Defense network had evolved over the decades. They had claimed their human genetic experiments were the first step, to preparing humans for extended space travel. Whether it was true or not, they had no way of being certain.

He wished Kaden hadn't explained some of the finer points of the Altered to her, but he understood. Team Three could be valuable allies to him.

"I'm not so much worried about me," she emphasized the last word.

"Mac, because he's different?" Hunter figured.

"Rafe and Wade were altered by the same laboratory."

Hunter raised his eyebrows at that. They stopped in front of the motel. "Kaden said the two of you were fourteenth gen."

"A joke, because we're all Wildblood. Hell, he can't even see Mac, so who knows. I think calling it fourteenth, or whatever, is what others say because we didn't understand better, and neither did they."

"Rafe saying it doesn't make it true."

"He only implied."

"I know; I was there." Hunter wanted to grab her and shake her, and tell her not to let Rafe get in her head. It was far too late for that. "You never answered my question."

"Short answer," she offered. "We can't do anything about Vance, the way things are."

"Oh, dear god," Hunter said, knowing what was coming next.

"So we're going to try to change the way things are. If the opportunity presents itself, Wade wants to attempt contacting Skolkovo."

"That's why you're out here, discovering the rest of the world. Making contacts and memorizing every little thing."

"You're thinking of Wade. I'm here as backup, sure, but he's on his own. I don't know where he is, or when he's going to talk to me again in any capacity. Neither does Mac. That's the way it is. I'll be made aware when it's important."

"I believe you," he said. "Is this what the three of you were planning in The Vista the last time?"

"No, Wade told us what he wanted to do. We talked him out of flying into Estes Park and assassinating Vance. This is a secondary plan."

Hunter shook his head. The same thing had happened when

Mac and Shan had been ambushed at the Junction. Rafe, and Wade had gone after him without considering the consequences. In time, it led them to Vance and Kaden. They discovered the ongoing conflict over the trade routes and territory boundaries, and that they weren't alone in the world. Or at least, the western half of the continent.

"For all the damned planning he talks about, he does a lot of dangerous things in the heat of the moment."

"You said it," she agreed. He unlocked their room door, tossed their packs on the bed, and ushered her in. Shan closed the door to continue the train of thought. "I've never spoken about this except to one other person, and it wasn't Mac. You cannot repeat it to anyone, ever." She had his attention. "Wade has a dark side, a violent side to him. You've never seen it. I have, but I can't elaborate, because of Security reasons."

The Blackout, five years ago. "Were you in danger?" His voice dropped, close to anger, fear, or both.

"Not from Wade. I felt the same calculated, emotionless response from Rafe during the assault on Manitou. Wade recognized the reaction, too. That's why I agreed to be on one of the teams out here. I'd rather be buttoned up in Angelfire for the winter, getting room service at your parents' chateau, but I can't ignore this."

Hunter was uncertain how he should react. It was the thing she was sworn to silence about. "Basically, you're his handler." He didn't understand how that would work for them and didn't want to.

"I suppose," she rubbed her eyes. She wandered into the bathroom, leaving her rifle propped in a corner. "Plumbing seems to work. I want to get a couple of hours sleep before we go out, I think."

"The heat is on," he said. "Sleep, in a bed — not a bad idea. Our conversation is over, then?"

"Security is out here to make a survey of the trade routes. If we make contact with Skolkovo, that's a plus, but they'll hear about us, if nothing else. Maybe they'll initiate contact, because we've made a name for ourselves. I'm here to keep Wade in line."

"Does he know?"

"It was his idea."

Chapter Eight

"I like what you've done with the place," Kyle made small talk. Unarmed except for a hunting knife tucked in his left boot; dressed in his best civilian clothes, black jeans, a gray shirt and jacket, he felt out of place. He understood what Shan had told him years ago about being in large gatherings back home. She was forever on guard, wondering if people might see things about her she didn't want them to see. He found it nerve-wracking.

As soon as he spoke, he wished he'd kept his mouth shut. Too late.

DeTessa regarded him for a moment before a wide smile crossed her face. "This isn't a test, young man, but a dinner to welcome you here. These events happen every weekend in the summer, but it's a rare treat this time of year." The meal had been delicious, rare roast beef with a mix of tender vegetables, freshly baked bread, butter, and a perfect crème brûlée dessert. Not extravagant, but impressive still.

"A test of sorts for us," he said. "We aren't used to new people, and those we've crossed haven't always been friendly."

"I understand. One reason we've established the center. There are so few of us, we can't afford to turn people away. Even those who aren't pleasant. Most have some redeeming qualities if you look closely enough. After all, how boring would life be if we were all alike?"

Kyle nodded, smiling back as his fellow Vistans mingled with other guests. The building, a three-story of gray stone, carried no distinguishing signs on the outside. The inside was all sleek glass and polished wood, plus large open spaces. He ignored the fact that it would be difficult as a defense point. If the Peacekeepers were worth anything, they were aware. "We didn't come south out of boredom."

"I doubt you came south from curiosity," she said.

"Not solely. This is Nebraska, and it was called the breadbasket of the continent for a reason."

"Are your people starving?" DeTessa asked bluntly.

"We've become self-sufficient, but we want to make sure it never becomes a problem again. Opening up trade seems to be the most viable of our options."

"This isn't the only group of your people out here in the winter?" She wore a long off-white silk dress for the evening, and her sidearm wasn't conspicuous. The tall, dark Peacekeeper shadowing her, was.

"This was planned so that we wouldn't be aware of others."

"Tell me why we should help you."

It was a test; he refrained. "Lambert is in charge. I can share my opinion. I can't speak for the rest of us, or for our village."

"Every opinion counts, and I like to hear the stories everyone has before I form my opinion."

"About me, or about us?"

She smiled. "We're all connected, and we have to learn to decipher how."

"Tell me your story," Kyle offered, "and I'll tell you mine."

"Join me for a drink, Mr. Taylor, and I'll tell you my story first. Then I'll tell you why."

"Kyle, please," he said, following her to a table. He pulled out her chair and waited for her to get comfortable before sitting next to her.

"I was born in a tiny seaside village south of Sao Paulo, Brasil, in the spring of 1989. My mother was young and alone, a common thing back then. Poverty was high, and jobs, especially for girls, were limited. She was quite smart, however, and made hard decisions. Once I was born, an aunt living in Canada 'adopted' me and brought her along as my nanny. Within a year, we had new names and a new home."

"That seems cut and dry."

"Oh, yes, now it's obvious," DeTessa admitted. A woman brought two dark green bottles from the bar and left them. "Too easy, but none of us recognized that for years." She saw she'd piqued his curiosity. "I was almost fifty years old when the war here broke out. Did you know I was that old?"

"It's not polite to ask, but no, I wouldn't have thought you were fifty now."

"A sincere observation. My only child, Marco, and I," she indicated the Peacekeeper standing not far away, "were living in Winnipeg, and realized we couldn't stay. The original plan was Mexico, and perhaps someday, Brasil."

"To go home, or to get across the equator?"

"There likely weren't as many nuclear hits as you think. We knew that whatever else happened, the farther south we moved, the safer we would be. In theory, because this is as far as we've traveled."

"Why here?"

"We had stopped here when the snow began. It didn't quit for months."

"April," Kyle said. He'd heard the story many times.

DeTessa nodded solemnly. "It all goes back to my adoption and defection. Do you know why we didn't die of the flu? There were fifty thousand refugees in the city, and that many people living here before. A tiny percentage of us survived until April."

"I have an idea."

"This is why you'll tell me your story when I'm finished with mine. I had discovered I was different quite by accident, as a child. A doctor got me into a group of children with similar differences. She had formed and organized an underground movement to help people like me. To make a long story short, a number of us had been left in society to see how we would develop. We didn't know what it was called then, and started using the name 'variant'. In time, it changed."

"To The Altered," Kyle said. "We've crossed enough places to hear the stories."

"Yes, although many names came after the public became aware we might exist."

"I'm sure I've heard some."

"You've met them before, too, even if you don't recognize them. It's not a straightforward thing."

Kyle nodded, wanting her to continue the story.

"The key to surviving after April would be trade, if anyone remained. Humans are resilient. We spent the next several years making this a place that the predatory among us would want to avoid."

"That couldn't have been easy."

"No. It was costly, in lives and resources. In a typical summer, we have close to twenty thousand people here. More than six thousand are permanent residents. I'm called an Elder because people trust my judgment, and because I'm old. To answer my question. The Altered among us were immune to the flu, at least the original, before the mutations began. Now tell me, what are your first memories? You're too young to have been born before the war."

"I suppose that depends on when you believe the war ended."

"You think the war has ended?" she asked. "The war here, not the war against the Altered, because they aren't the same."

"I was born in December of '37," he said, digesting the implications.

She waited before answering, as if she held a well-kept secret. He could ask anyone. "The war was over almost as soon as it had begun.

All the smaller ones, in July. August, more, bigger, nuclear. I'm certain your people have their own stories, as we do. Many are written down, if you'd care to read them, and if you stay that long."

"I think we will, and I'd be interested in reading what you have to say."

"Not just me, but hundreds of accounts, perhaps thousands by now. We invite people to share."

Kyle sat back, enjoying the lager — smooth, crisp in flavor, and cold. "I remember the snow being almost constant in the mountains. Of all the frightening things to recall, the one good memory that stands out is that there was always someone there to tell us everything would be all right. They kept us as safe as they could."

"That is important. Tell me about your sister."

He nodded towards Chris. "My brother."

"We discussed my heritage. I saw what you are, what she is, the moment we met." DeTessa wasn't insulted or impatient. If he hadn't attempted to deny it, she'd have wondered why. "It's the reason you are here. I suspected something when we first communicated with each other."

"I'm not an Altered," he told her.

"Don't take this as an insult; it's an observation. You were a control. Your twin is the Altered. While I sense this, others wouldn't unless they knew what it was to begin with. You are the counteractant, the opposite. Perhaps because you were born so late, she is a Wildblood."

"Meaning what?"

"She is conscious of her abilities."

"I'm here to negotiate trade. As I've said, I don't speak for others. It's not my place."

"Then tell me what you can about you."

He smiled at that, seeing she'd maneuvered him right where she wanted. "It's going to be less exciting than watching the snow fall."

"You might surprise yourself."

"I'll take inventory of our supplies in the morning," Hunter said, holding the door to the way station open for her. They'd been frugal, but if they had a chance to stock up, he'd grab it, even if it meant getting another pack horse. Nebraska in the winter was nothing to be trifled with.

"The weather report looks decent a week out. If it doesn't change, we might swing farther south and see the sights." Shan noticed the dining area was less crowded than the past few nights. Their food might get to them quicker. Talking with the locals was fascinating, so she didn't mind waiting a few extra minutes for a hot meal.

"Let's not get too far off the interstate. Weather reports aren't what they used to be. We can find the Platte River Center if we can find the highway."

"I don't expect there's a lot to see out here."

"Not before, not now."

Ester and Harvey, the proprietors, in the kitchen and behind the bar late in the day, were missing. "Where is everyone?" There were three men standing by the rear fire doors, and no one else. She repeated the question loudly enough for them to hear her.

One came forward. "There are raiders out near the stables, heading this way. We're gathering people to chase them off."

Stable, homes, way station, in that order. She'd seen the hand-drawn map of the town.

"We left the big guns in our room," Hunter said.

"It might be better if you stay back. Keep her out of the way," another of them said.

Hunter could practically hear her eyes roll and spoke up before she did. "Where we're from, she's a cop. So am I. If you need help, say so."

"Cops?"

"Security and Scout officers."

"Sure, I get what you mean. I didn't expect it from you."

"I did," Harvey answered, coming out of the back, shotgun in hand. "They talk like cops, they act like cops." They said they were from Angelfire, too. Rumor was, the Senator had an army up in the mountains, and was cleaning out the more aggressive gangs. It had been all the talk last summer, and now, here they were.

Shan shrugged when Hunter stole a glance at her.

"It's going to be dark soon," Harvey went on. "That's a big disadvantage."

"We've been trained to take care of this sort of problem."

"Would you lend us a hand?" Harvey asked. "We don't have a permanent police force, and the only training we've had is dealing with these assholes a couple of times a year."

Hunter didn't even try not to grin at that.

"We'll be back in two minutes," Shan answered, figuring the men would discuss it to death, or until it was irrelevant. When they returned, they each dropped a duffel bag on the bar and began pulling out guns and various other bits of equipment. Night vision goggles, Kevlar vests, knives.

"Where's your wife?" one man asked Harvey as they watched.

"In the back, doing the same. If you go through the kitchen, you'd better call out and let her know. Otherwise, buckshot," Harvey warned.

"What do you do when they show up?" Hunter asked.

"We go out and shoot at them; they shoot at us. Sometimes they burn houses. Sometimes, people get killed." He looked at Shannon. "Pretty soon they'll get bored and move on down the road. A few hours, maybe less, because there are no traders here to harass. I don't recognize this bunch, so there's no telling."

"How open to suggestions are you?"

"Let's hear what you have to say, but we don't have a lot of time."

"More than you might think," Shan said. "Let them come to us."

"Here, in the station?" Harvey asked, speaking for all of them.

"It's bound to put them off balance when you change your tactics," Hunter filled in the details. "Then we tell them why they don't want to come back here and make trouble for you, or for the Angelfire Assembly."

Harvey thought it over. "What if they decide to shoot us instead?"

"That's not going to happen. You don't think we came out here clueless and untrained?" Hunter knew it wouldn't appease them, so he had a backup plan. "But if things go sideways, get down and stay there. Tell everyone to keep out of sight until you say otherwise."

Harvey motioned for the others to get moving. "It won't be more than a few minutes." He looked worried. "There's a dozen of them. I'd rather not have to bury you."

"Be as neutral as you can when they get here. Appease them. I'll do the talking. She backs me up."

"And this works?"

"It always has before," Hunter lied. It got them out of the diner.

"Where do you want to do this?" Shan asked the moment they were alone.

"Are we talking or shooting?"

"Talk, to begin with. You're familiar with the routine."

"Follow your lead."

She nodded. "This time, I'm going to follow your lead. Give them the opportunity to get the hell out of town alive, but take no shit. Let's move these tables closer to the walls. I want them in the center of the room, and I want cover if we need it."

"Old tables aren't my first choice, but it could be worse."

"They're heavy and more a distraction than cover." Shan caught him watching her. "Unless you have a better idea."

"No, grab an end," he said, helping her with the furniture.

"They're out in the front lot," one of the local men reported as they retreated inside. "They'll follow us."

"Good," Hunter said. "Stay on the kitchen side, stay visible unless, you know. Shoot out." He sat on the edge of a table, a holstered .45 on his left shoulder. Shannon stood next to him, to his left, arms crossed, face unreadable, a Sig 9mm in her right hand. Its twin was holstered on her right shoulder. Her hair was up in a pony-tail, and he didn't like how young she looked, or how female. It was part of the ploy.

A group of men clamored in the doorway, milling around. Six of them, and from the way they moved, some had been drinking. After a disjointed discussion that grew into an argument, one of them strode forward, checking their surroundings.

"So, the truck stop is under new management?" a tall, blond, unshaven man of about thirty asked, both sarcastic and amused. He was armed, as they all were, but he didn't appear to be one of the inebriated.

Shannon pursed her lips and gave a slight nod.

"And, ah, you speak for them?" He ventured closer, eyeing Hunter, then her.

"I do." Hunter said.

She wanted to ask him if he always started sentences with conjunctions, but she doubted he'd understand.

"I'm here to give you a choice, because the 'new management' prefers to start out on the right foot," Hunter said.

"What sort of choice?" Taking note of the armed men in the kitchen, he glanced back at his people. They understood.

"If we are cordial or not."

He tipped his head, perhaps annoyed at the inconvenience of having to talk about why they were there.

"We don't have to be. In fact, most people don't get to make that choice for themselves. My employers usually decide on how to deal with outlanders, with Nomads."

"They sent you to threaten us?" he spoke in lower tones, the initial amusement wearing off.

"I can change my mind about how nice we are."

Silence.

"What choice?" he finally asked.

"New management has a name, and it's the Angelfire Assembly."

"If I knew who that was, would it make a difference?"

Shannon was aware he was outright lying. She clicked her tongue and sighed.

"What's your name?" Hunter asked, understanding what she didn't say.

"My name?" he repeated. "I'm Ryan, not that it means anything to you."

"Just Ryan?"

"Yeah, just Ryan."

"The reason you get a choice is because the Assembly has never heard of you. You haven't made a name for yourself out here, harassing farmers. If you had, if they knew your name, this would have been over about five seconds after you walked through the front door."

Shan tapped her trigger finger on the side of her Sig.

"You think she could have shot all of us, and we'd stand there?"

"The five of us could have eliminated the six of you without even one of you getting a shot off. It's cold out, and you've likely been riding since first light. Tired, drunk, cold, while we're all warm, rested, and ready for you."

"What do you want?" the Nomad in charge asked.

"Senator Caulder feels enough is enough. He wants people to have a second chance. Now I know your name. If you come back here and cause trouble, you lose the choice to ride away a free man. If you come back here and want to eat, sleep, drink, trade, or just play cards, all is forgiven."

"What if I shoot you, and Caulder never knows my name? What if we shoot all of you and burn the station, as a warning to the high and mighty up there in the mountains?"

"You told him your name," Shan said.

"What? Yeah, I told him my name. So the hell what? They are five hundred miles away. To you, they might as well be on the moon."

"Never tell someone your name," she offered. "Until you understand their intentions."

"Is there a particular reason he keeps you close?" Ryan leered.

Shan tipped her head up and stared straight at him.

"Bodyguard," Hunter said. "Take that any way you want. I'm still alive."

"For now."

"The thing is, we just work for them. We aren't from Angelfire; we don't live there. We can't, but they're more than happy to pay us for our services." He let that sink in, to whatever ends they might assume.

"Trying to make me think you're one of the mutant freaks the rich folks use for their dirty work doesn't scare me. I recognize them when I see them."

"The hell you do," Shan said it quietly enough that the men hanging back by the doors couldn't hear her.

"Little girl, you have no idea."

Hunter let her go. If they even breathed wrong, he was going to take it on himself to start that shootout he'd promised to try to avoid.

"I've seen things with my own eyes that happened before I was born," she said, leaning towards him, stoic. "I've killed my kind for threatening me, and I've hunted fucking Nomads who thought they'd outsmarted me, and I never thought twice about them. If you make us slaughter the entire bunch of you, I won't remember your face tomorrow."

Ryan blinked, thinking of something to say, convinced she was trying to scare him with horror stories, and it didn't work. It mostly didn't work.

"One bit of advice," she finished. "It's not 'mutant freak', it's 'Altered'. Other humans did this to us on purpose, and we didn't get a choice. Altered is even a slur now. Be careful what you say, because some of us are touchy."

"But not you?"

"Not about that."

Hunter felt the change in her when she started the barrage. He felt it again as she took a cleansing breath to make it stop. He didn't understand why, if they were about to go to guns with the Nomads.

"Pick your poison," she said, "or maybe ask the guy that runs this place if you can get a real fucking job. They need some muscle to keep the riffraff away."

"Are you calling me riffraff?" Ryan asked, but the tension was gone out of his voice.

"You were waving a shotgun at a bunch of old men playing cards on the porch. No, nice people do shit like that all the time." Sarcastic rather than aggressive.

It occurred to Hunter that he didn't like this Nomad smiling at her. He cleared his throat and stood. Ryan was taller and broader. He didn't care. "Are we shooting each other, or having supper?"

"What's for supper?" Ryan asked.

"Rabbit stew or venison steak. I didn't see what side dishes we have because you damned raiders interrupted," Harvey called out from the kitchen.

"Is that a genuine invitation?"

"If it weren't, you wouldn't be in a position to worry." Shan wandered off behind the bar to get a bottle. Whiskey. It was easy to understand why Mac drank. Not so much recently, but once upon a time, it could have grown into a real problem. "Work out the details with Harvey. It's his place."

"You old enough to be drinking hard liquor?" Ryan followed her to the bar, attempting a joke.

Hunter stopped next to him. "Really?"

She took a swig right from the almost empty bottle, wandering to a table, ignoring the men, knowing the direction of the conversation they were about to have. "I owe you, Harvey."

"The hell you do," he called back.

"So, the truck stop needs people," Ryan repeated as Hunter set them up a round of drinks. The rest of his men scattered, some retreating outside, others finding seats as the locals spread the word the fight was over. The place would be back to its version of normal in half an hour. "I don't suppose putting up a 'Help Wanted' sign out front does much good."

"How many of you are there?"

"Twenty-seven, counting the women and kids. Can they support all of us in the winter?"

"We can," Ester brought bowls of stew over. "There's work, and in the spring, the smaller campgrounds need people more than we do. It's not easy, but it's honest."

"Ouch," Hunter offered.

"I have no designs on your woman," Ryan told him. "I didn't mean to imply that, but you get a look in your eyes that says you'd kill anyone that gave her a sideways glance."

"It's not quite that bad."

"I have a wife, I understand. Do you work for the people in Angelfire?"

"We do."

"They aren't fans of the mut... The Altered."

"Very aware. Our working relationship is unique for reasons I won't discuss. Trust me when I say you're lucky you ran across us rather than some of the others."

"They hunt your kind."

"We found that out the hard way. She hopes there is redemption in people. Not all of us share the sentiment."

"Do you?" It was a simple question. The answer never would be.

"I think everyone deserves a second chance, because few things can't be forgiven. A year ago, she wouldn't have given you that. Neither would I. Things change. Don't make us regret the decision."

"We've been on the road so long," Ryan started. He stopped, not trusting his voice. "I was a kid when the war happened."

"Yeah, me too," Hunter confessed. "You won't mention the details of our conversation, because you're right. I'd kill anyone who messed with her."

"I don't know what you mean."

Hunter nodded. "We're heading for North Platte when the weather looks good. If any of your people want to join us, they're welcome to tag along."

"Safety in numbers?"

"Sometimes," Hunter said. "Just bigger trouble."

"Care to explain what in the hell?" Hunter stalked into the room, letting the door slam behind him. He'd followed her out of the way station like he had a purpose. Shan was already discarding her gear across the spare bed. In a minute, she'd be naked, and he'd be distracted.

"I need a shower," she answered. "Give me five."

"You never take a five-minute shower." He got to the hallway and blocked her way to the bathroom. "That was not normal. That wasn't you. What in the hell?"

"When I get the words right, I'll explain."

"Shan, don't do this on your own."

"I'm not. You're here. Don't ask me right now. Some things don't have words."

"We can figure it out." He spoke too late, and as she moved past him, the light flickered in the back, and he heard the shower turn on. "Keep in mind, the water is solar heated." Meaning, she'd be lucky if she had five minutes of hot water. He stripped off his gear, wondering if it had ever been a good idea to wander out on the trade routes. There were too many variables for any of them to be safe. He was afraid of losing her or worse, putting her in danger because he was stupid.

She threw a damp towel at him four minutes later, hair wet, dressed in flannel pants and a tee shirt that used to be his. Gray wasn't her favorite color, but it was that or winter camo. "Go ahead."

"What happened over there? You never tell people who you are, what you are."

"If we had gone on seconds longer, they'd be burying people instead of serving them drinks and supper. I'm tired of doing this because I don't understand why anymore. Those people, they're trying to survive the only way they've ever known."

"I get that. We were all pretty twitchy, including you. It's not what I meant, and you know it."

"It wasn't me," she shrugged.

"No shit. Wait, what do you mean, it wasn't you?"

"I said it, but those weren't my words. I was improvising."

"Wade. It's what you tried to tell me about when we got here." He'd always known she was omitting things about the team.

"That you aren't supposed to repeat."

"Talking to you doesn't break the promise."

"No," she agreed. "I've seen things from the past, you know that. Ghosts. And I pulled the trigger on Rafe, so to speak."

He'd been standing next to her when she called for the strike. "What about the torturing Nomads? Does Security Command condone that?"

"Not even close. When the Nomads firebombed Depot South during the Blackout."

"Wade?"

"Yes, but more people than he and I are implicated."

"And you're okay with this?"

"It happened in the middle of a firefight. I was days out of training, and controlling him isn't a simple matter."

"One time, Shan, isn't likely."

"Do you think I don't know that? The other thing — and this is a euphemism, so don't read anything into it. While I was channeling Wade and a few minutes later, when I had some whiskey. Both events are what I warned you about when I tried to explain what I was, way back when. Extreme emotions can trigger my abilities. Now I'm aware of where Wade is, now I know where Mac is. And vice versa."

"No shit," he said after a moment. "Why isn't Mac in Cody?"

"No idea. We're heading for North Platte anyway, and maybe someone can answer our questions."

"Are they there now?"

"No. I think that's the place to be this spring, though, and Wade is on his way. He won't tell me what happened at The Vista after we scattered. He hasn't been home since. Neither has a lot of people associated with the 'Conda."

"They're in Cody."

"Yes. I don't have the option of going home."

"Do you think Council and Command had it out?"

She pursed her lips, shaking her head. "There is no way I'd make a guess about what happened. They didn't tell Mac details either."

"Would you tell me if he told you?"

Shan nodded. "I have nothing to hide from you, and I might be asking your family for asylum."

"I'll take you anywhere to be safe."

"That's not the goal right now."

"When it is, say the word." Hunter didn't want her to mistake his caution for hesitation.

"What if we don't know where a safe place is?" Shan had never felt comfortable, safe, not even as a child. Nothing had changed.

"We'll look until we find something that we can make safe. I never expected life with you to be easy."

"This one time, I'd like to have disappointed you."

Chapter Nine

Nebraska mid morning March 2

"We have new orders," Lambert announced, not caring that he was interrupting breakfast. It happened. The rest of the day didn't look much better.

"From who?" Chris asked.

"Whom," Kyle corrected. "From whom?"

Before they got into another spat, Lambert crossed his arms and cleared his throat. "From Wade." Sibling rivalry was a thing, an annoying as hell thing.

He had their attention.

"I'd expect he would contact me," Kyle said. "Not arguing, stating a fact." He hadn't shared his conversation with DeTessa. If it were true, he wouldn't have a choice in the matter. He'd be recalled. He could go home. First, he had to talk to Wade in person, and Shannon, if she would listen. There was a 50/50 chance.

"I'll get to that, too. The team from Black Hills started south about the same time we did. They might be one of the groups that arrived overnight. Wade said Yates is bringing them here."

"I thought Yates was one of the dead ex-partners of Vance's."

"You're going to love this," Lambert said, meaning he was not. "Yates is a long way from gone; he's here, and Kaden is with him. He calls himself Harlan now. Our mistake, not something Team Three missed. He's as hunted as they are."

"Hunted?" Cassie repeated.

"The Altered were trained to hunt other Altered. Rival corporations, for whatever reason. They still do it when the opportunity arises."

"It's what happened to Team Three at The Junction," Kyle said, voice dropping. He'd been first on the scene, and sometimes, he had nightmares about it. They'd almost lost Mac. It was the finale in a series of events that had led them to Nebraska.

"Yeah," Lambert agreed. "We don't know their objectives. Trade routes, sure. The safety net up north. Beyond that, there's more; there has been since before all this started. Back to The Blackout, maybe farther. The team didn't tell us, and there has to be a damned good reason."

"What's your point?"

"We're going to find out soon. It's going to shock us into seeing things a whole lot differently than we do now. Or so I've been told."

"Why does that scare me?" Kyle said.

"Because you're close to them. They could come out of left field with something we never expected. That's why Wade hasn't contacted you. After all this, they're still distancing themselves. To me, it means what Rafe started isn't over," Lambert said. "They don't want us here, but there might come a time we are needed. Backup and such. An important reason we need to understand the laws here."

"Great."

"Tell me they don't have warheads," Cassie added.

They all looked at Lambert. "I asked about that. Shannon swears it can't happen, that it was a fluke. Wade said all of us will be here within the week, if the river don't rise."

"What does that mean?"

"I think it's safer not to ask."

"How did he contact you?" Kyle was curious, knowing it had to be conventional.

"When I wast out for my jog down the lakefront, a Peace-keeper came along and told me I had a message at the radio station."

"He saw we were here."

"Or he was guessing?" Chris speculated.

"You've worked with them. They do little guesswork. He knew we were here; hell, he may be here himself. Keep your eyes open and be careful. If he's here, it's easy to imagine not-so-friendly people were too. What happened a year ago was bad, and they didn't make friends in Colorado." Lambert didn't have the details, so he couldn't give up secrets. The Blackout was another story.

"Are we ever going to be told what happened?"

"No," Kyle stated.

"They don't joke about 'no one knows everything', do they?" Chris asked.

"Not even a little."

"Why are we here?" Kyle asked. "Team Three doesn't need us to negotiate trade routes."

"The only alternative I can think of is backup," Lambert offered. "Like I said, like it's always been."

"Or Angelfire has figured them out."

"We can't negotiate anything if they won't let us into the city."

"I keep asking myself, why did Rafe leave them alone for years? Why did he show up, in The Vista? What triggered it?"

"You have an idea."

"The spring Sweeps, when they said they went to Cody. More sealed files. Where did they really go? Where did Shan and Green go the summer before?" Kyle shrugged. "Someone had to have gone to NORAD. Vance didn't help us set up the assault on Manitou, and they already knew what they needed."

"Sweeps, by accident or on purpose, shook Rafe out of hiding, and he decided he'd waited long enough to hunt them."

Kyle wasn't satisfied with that. "We're missing something."

"Yeah," Lambert agreed. "Maybe we should leave it that way."

"I may not be Altered, but she's my sister. We all grew up together. Some of that influence is mine."

"I forget that. Keep reminding me, because it might come in handy."

"We need to get a fucking clue about why we're here. I'm not afraid to ask."

"The job is yours," Lambert told him. "Those new orders. We're supposed to contact the Black Hills delegation, if we can, and arrange to move the meeting place from here. This place might not be as neutral as we hoped."

The competition was intense, hours long, and winding down as only nine of the original participants had the stamina to still be there at daybreak. At nightfall, the events had begun with an extensive obstacle course that cleared them out by half. The rest of the games were inside with an audience. Southwest of the occupied parts of the city, the casino kept the loudest and rowdiest of its activities contained.

It was Henderson's turn to pick an opponent. Tall, black, with a high and tight buzz-cut, smooth gray leather pants; a silk shirt in baby blue between rounds and a tight white tee shirt and jeans while participating. He knew women appreciated a man who took care of himself and made it look easy to look good.

He cocked his head to one side, distracted, and the corner of his mouth twitched in what could be interpreted as a smile. "Good morning, young lady," he greeted in his rich baritone voice. "What can I do for you?"

Wade had known she was there before anyone looked up. Angry, certainly. Other than that, it remained to be seen how she would react.

It didn't take long. Shannon kicked the back leg of his chair, forcing the front legs to the floor, making him sit up and pay attention.

"Where have you been?" she glared, arms crossed. If he hadn't shaved off his dark hair, leaving only a shadow, if he wasn't hiding behind mirrored glasses, smoking a cigar, and drinking a tall glass of whiskey, she'd have found him faster. A holiday of some sort, and there had to be close to four hundred people crowded into the casino at this ungodly hour. "Geoffrey," she added. Wade wasn't a safe name to use.

"Geoffrey," one of the other men snickered, cutting it off as she shot him a glare. The rest kept comments to themselves, controlling their amusement. Shan wore winter camos that fit her well; a tall woman with emerald green eyes and dark wavy hair held back in a long ponytail. It looked like she was packing a gun under her parka, too. Interesting, if nothing else, but easy to look at, pissed off or not.

"You might have let me know you were still fucking alive," she spat.

"I didn't expect to be gone this long."

"How long have you been here?"

Wade pretended to peer at a watch he wasn't wearing. "About fourteen hours."

"I meant Nebraska. North Platte, the Platte River Center. Here," she repeated, exasperated.

"A few days. Time gets away when you're snowed in."

"That's your excuse? You could have gotten word to me."

Putting the cigar down, he stood. "I'm sorry." Henderson had been about to pick him as an opponent for the next round. Arm wrestling first. His choice next. Wade nodded at the group, not caring if the spectators were restless. The competition wasn't the only event in the building. "One minute." He took her by the forearm.

"One minute," Henderson repeated, watching.

"Who else is here?"

"None of your business." Angry and relieved, but mostly angry.

"It is. We can talk about it later."

Shan pulled her arm away. "When you feel like it?"

"Can you give me a couple more hours?"

"Why not?" She shrugged with an exaggerated arm wave. "We've got a cabin at the Oak Lane Court, in the city. I'm sure you can figure out where that is."

"Who's 'we'?"

"Find out in a couple of hours, if you can bother."

"Don't be mad," Wade attempted to appease her.

"Mad? You've seen me mad, and this isn't even close."

She was furious. "I'm sorry." The words sounded less sincere than they were, and he hoped it wouldn't trigger her into doing something irrational. She was supposed to be the voice of reason, the calm and collected one. The idea made him smile.

"This isn't funny."

"No, it's not, and I'm sorry I let things go on this long. I'll try not to let it happen again."

"That's a shitty attempt at a promise. I don't know why I walked all the way out here to see you. My mistake again." She sighed. "The rest of you gentlemen, have a nice day." She stalked away, finished.

They watched, someone offering a low whistle.

"Don't," Wade warned, taking his seat.

"She is angry," Henderson emphasized. "And..."

"Really, don't," Wade repeated. "My sister," he emphasized.

"I'm sorry," Henderson offered. "That has to be rough, having a sister that looks like that, and men being the way we are."

"I've only had to kill a couple of men for her. She usually handles it herself." He got back to the game at hand. The tone of his voice told that he wasn't joking.

"I believe you. Put in a word for me anyway? Just a nice, quiet dinner somewhere not here." Henderson tried to make the situation less tense.

"Not happening. She knows how stupid men act about her, and she's here with someone. A male someone." He wasn't certain of whom, but not Mac. There were a couple of other possibilities.

Henderson wagged his eyebrows. "That's too bad. Let's hit the ring and see who pays for the next round of drinks."

"I thought we were arm wrestling."

"Changed my mind," Henderson grinned. "I don't think this is the last beating you'll be getting today."

When she got to the double doors at the north exit, two Peacekeepers standing there. They looked like they were waiting for her. "Ma'am," one of them stepped forward, not threatening but curious. She didn't feel the urge to go on the defensive.

"Can I help you?" Shan put her hands on her hips, keeping them visible.

"I'm Officer Ueda. This is Officer Ricci."

"I'm Capt. Allen," she said.

He paused for a moment. "Are you Shannon Allen?"

"I am. Are you here to arrest me?"

"Have you broken any laws?" Ueda asked, a bit confused.

"No, not that I'm aware of. Why are you looking for me?"

"The Elders have asked to speak with you. We're delivering the message."

"When and where?"

"Now. At the Market Square."

"I have previous commitments." She tried to get out of an immediate confrontation, alone. They'd been in the city all of five hours, and it had taken her two to find someone going out to the casino. She'd only walked halfway.

"It won't take long," Ueda assured her.

There was an outburst of shouts from a band of workers on the south road. "What in the hell?" Ricci exclaimed, grabbing his binoculars to have a look.

"Well?" Shan asked, impatient, knowing what the chances were it wasn't a serious thing.

"Riders," Ricci barked out. "A lot of them cresting the far ridgeline." Ueda was on his radio, calling for reinforcements.

"How far out are they?" she asked. Shan threw a mental warning to Wade because he'd understand. It had been less than two days since she'd known where he was. This was no coincidence. They were Nomads, looking for him and maybe her.

"Five minutes," Ueda said. "Ten if we're lucky, and there's still a lot of mud out there. Sometimes they run trucks up the interstate, medium-sized ones because semis get stuck. The roads aren't what they used to be. They recognize it scares people. It doesn't work so well since we started shooting back, but they still remind us they're out there."

"You should take shelter inside," Ricci warned. "They won't come across the road; they understand we patrol here."

"Where is your backup?" Shan needed to know their options. The riders were absolutely going to cross the road. "Just in case things are different today."

"Once they call a muster at the barracks, they'll be here in ten minutes," Ueda said.

Neutral ground. "Pull the fire alarm."

"What?"

"A building that big has to have some sort of alarm system."

"I know what you said. It'll cause a panic," Ueda argued.

"No, it will call our support teams in," Ricci said. "Maybe give us a fighting chance if they cross the road."

Wade burst through the doors, Henderson on his heels, both armed and in tactical gear they hadn't been wearing a few minutes earlier.

"How many of them?" She asked, so everyone would know.

"Twenty, give or take," Wade said.

"We have a fighting chance," she said. "South."

"I wish I had a sniper rifle with me."

"We have four in our SUV," Ricci said. "Right around the corner."

"Four?" Wade was willing to share. "What kind?"

".308 Winchesters."

"An SUV," Shan added. Before she'd been displaced into the outlands, she'd been a Scout, and driving was what she did.

"I absolutely forbid you from taking a vehicle out there and engaging them," Wade left no room for discussion.

"This is what we do."

"And this isn't The Vista."

"And you don't get to tell me what to do anymore," she pointed out, voice ratcheting up. "But we'll do it your way, for now." It was a lie, and they both were aware.

"I'm the officer in charge," Ueda spoke.

"Between the two of us," Shan said, "we have fifteen years' experience in dealing with Nomads, raiders. Them," she pointed. "They're here because we are. We didn't think they'd follow us here, and not on the same damned day."

"Do it; I'll take the responsibility," Ricci decided. "I'm setting off the fire call inside, and I'll keep the crowd calm. Get the guns."

"Hell yeah," Henderson agreed.

Ueda popped the hatchback open. "This could get me fired."

"This could keep you alive," Wade said. "You and lots of other people in the casino."

"That's nice, I'm not a sniper," Shan grimaced, remembering a shootout at Depot North, back home, when she'd first met Hunter. She was definitely not a sniper, and he took pleasure in teasing her about it.

Slapping a panel open, Ueda revealed a rack of handguns.

"This will work," she nodded in approval.

"I thought you'd developed an aversion to killing," Wade said to her.

"You know why they're here. It's not by accident. They followed us, they tracked us, even after all this time. We were minding our own damned business. This isn't just about us anymore."

"My point," Wade agreed. "I'm glad you see it."

"We still have things to discuss." A klaxon sounded somewhere inside the casino.

"Maybe later, over drinks," Henderson helped himself to a pair of .45s. "Nice. I'm supposed to watch your back," he told her.

Shan picked out a second pair of 9mms and stuffed them in her parka pockets. "Great. Try to keep up. I'm not a sniper."

"What does that mean?" Ueda and Henderson asked at the same time.

"She's going right out there to see what sort of mess we're in. Any of them who get close, that's their problem. 'Keep your head down' means nothing to her." Wade watched as she made her way out, knowing how easily she could blend into the landscape. It was a talent. It was her talent, and let her go.

The road hadn't been maintained, and low scrub brush made the way rough. There was enough of an embankment left to provide a place to wait, considering how flat everything she'd seen for a few hundred miles was. "I don't need a babysitter," she told Henderson, finding a culvert pipe and pulling debris out of the way.

"He said to tell you to 'shut the fuck up and deal with it' if you protested."

Shan peered at him. "Who said 'shut the fuck up'?" She hadn't heard Wade say five curse words in his entire life.

"Halley, your brother. You remember him, right?"

His made-up name. She raised an eyebrow. "Wade."

"Wade," he repeated. "He's Wade...."

"I'm Allen, and you walked into a mess, because Wade didn't ask you to follow me. Did Kaden tell you what to expect, at least?" She'd known, from the moment he spoke to her, why he was there. The extent of his motives was another matter.

"Wildblood. You just proved it. Who is Kaden?"

She snorted, easing closer to the wall of dirt, the rumble of vehicles moving closer. "Let them pass unless they see us."

"This isn't my first rodeo. You want to catch them in the crossfire. Grand plan, as long as we don't get caught in the crossfire."

Arming herself, she crouched down, watching the Nomads move in. Henderson followed suit. There was fire from their snipers at the casino. Or Peacekeepers. A handful of riders crossed the road a quarter mile east, loud and uncoordinated.

"Let them go," she whispered. "Where are your friends?"

"Close, I hope, if they heard the alarm."

"I don't need your help. You don't want to hear what I think, because all of it's rude."

He sat back on his heels, smiling. "Is that what they tell you?"

"All the time. When I figure out which one of these Nomads is tracking us, I'm putting a couple of bullets in his brain."

"Or wing him, and interrogate him later."

"That never works out quite right."

"I don't think we're going to have to wait." He tensed.

Riders crossed the road east and west of them, more milling around just beyond the embankment. A negative shake of her head indicated she wasn't planning on starting a firefight.

"Shit," Henderson groaned, knowing there would be hell to pay. He'd been told to keep them updated on Team Three. A simple task. Wade wasn't supposed to be Halley. She wasn't supposed to be in Nebraska, and it had been a fluke he recognized her. He looked around to see if any of his men were close, in case he needed a hand. No such luck.

Shan had an instantaneous flash of warning and turned on Henderson. He was fast, part of the reason he'd been chosen for the assignment. She managed to stop him dead in his tracks for a moment, but he'd already fired. The girl was right; things never went the way they were supposed to. Two of the stun gun's four wireless electrodes missed her. The other two connected, hitting her high in the chest, where she'd had her parka open to get to her clips. It only slowed her down. She dropped and rolled away, but by the time she had control of the disorientation that washed over her, Henderson was gone.

Wade realized the misjudgment they'd both made, too. It was half-a-mile back across open ground. She wouldn't try to come in now, with plenty of daylight left. He wondered whose path they'd crossed.

"Those are the Sixth," Ueda announced, peering through his scope.

"Which ones?" Wade didn't want to shed blood with potential allies, but it might already be too late.

"Damned if I know. There are at least two clans messing around, and it's not the first time we've seen them," he gestured towards the east. "Sooner or later, someone is going to get killed, then the Peacekeepers will step in."

"They want to draw us out," Wade said. "Us, not you."

"It worked."

"Not like they hoped."

Lambert watched the riders scatter as new intruders appeared. One of them had a massive snowplow welded to the front of a jeep; digging ruts in the mud and running at the frightened horses. They had learned that no one with any authority would bother them as long as they left the travelers be. For the most part, they let the travelers be.

"Shoot his fucking tires out," Kaden urged, watching through binoculars. He liked horses more than most people.

"You're an observer," Lambert reminded him. "I didn't hear a word you said," he offered, getting comfortable with the Barrett .50 caliber. "Be ready to move, because this is going to piss them off." At the bottom of the hill, Tero looked nervous, holding their horses.

One shot did it, blasting through the unprotected rear driver's side tire, and the machine limped along, lurching to a halt.

"Come on," Kaden grinned, grabbing the tripod and heading for the horses.

"They can't zero in on us with one shot."

"Yeah, that's great. We're still not supposed to engage. Besides, I smell smoke. They like to set fires to make us break cover."

"Do you mean scare them off, or end them?" Lambert wondered, not having worked with him before. The Sixth, for all the rumor and innuendo, were far more passive than the rest of the world gave them credit for. He packed the rifle away. He wasn't a sniper either.

"Whatever is called for. These are clansmen showing off their firepower. You call them Nomads. Some of them are aware some of us are here." They mounted up and headed north, towards the interstate.

"You wonder if I could be one of you. The Gen En," Lambert said.

"I keep thinking that about everyone I meet from The Vista. We're allies, so there's supposed to be some trust here. I mean, you know what I am."

"Telling serves your purpose. People are wary of you; people avoid you because of lies they heard before you were born. You're an enforcer. It makes it easier for you to intimidate them. We were isolated. Everyone in The Vista knows everyone else. There was no room for error."

"So, no matter what you admit to, I can't believe you?"

"You didn't come out of Montana with me. Trust is earned. Ask me again later."

"In ten years?" Kaden joked.

"Sure. Time to deal with these amateurs." Lambert pulled on a pair of leather gloves, adjusting his gear, knowing Team Three dressed alike for a reason. If they were going to make a statement, they were going to go big. "Keep in mind, we don't want a blood-spattered mess out here. It's a fine point. We want to help unite the trade routes, not rip them apart in border wars and meaningless squabbles over who owns what."

"That's your point," Tero spoke. "We own nothing. This place, this planet, this existence, could snuff us out in an instant."

Lambert knew how true that was from firsthand experience. He nodded. "One of us, or all of us. We do what we expect is right, and hope we are."

"Good philosophy. Let's go roust some outlanders," Kaden said. This particular Vistan was more amiable than Wade, and even Shannon. In Kaden's mind, that made him as dangerous, Altered or not.

"Make a lot of noise, waste your ammo. We're here to attract their attention. The window we need isn't extended."

"You'll see if we made sufficient distractions," Kaden said, still prying for any clue.

"That's up to Team Three to take advantage or not."

"You're here to make sure they have someplace safe to retreat to." They both knew he meant not only Platte River, but Cody.

"That I am." They cleared the crest of the hill and could see a game of cat-and-mouse unfolding across the snowy fields. It looked like a display, like a distraction. Like what they were doing. "We're on," Lambert repeated. "Let's give them a show."

Kaden took his advice, charging out onto the road like he had a plan.

"What did you expect he was going to do?" Tero asked, trying to keep up. "He knows why we're out here."

"I hope so. We've had long discussions about our priorities and our motives."

"They aren't like people were even a generation ago. That's what happens when you play with genetics. Too many variables."

"So I hear."

"Maybe Kaden is wrong about you, and right about one of the others. Taylor or MacKenzie. Someone you've kept hidden away in The Vista."

Lambert knew there were many hidden away in The Vista.

People who had no clue they were different, and as far as anyone had determined, therefore inactive. No special abilities. He ignored the prompt, still amused they considered he might be Gen En.

"Are you hiding from that girl?" Kaden emphasized the last word, taunting someone as they caught up, hitting another low gully.

Henderson turned, aiming a big handgun at Kaden. Lambert and Tero both drew on the outlander. They all stared at each other for a long moment. "Kai?" he said, hesitating. "Aren't you supposed to be about ten?"

"Ten years ago," Kaden agreed. "You're not supposed to be this far east."

"You realize why I am." Henderson eyed his companions, recognizing neither. "And you're damned right I'm hiding from that 'girl'."

"She's the reason we're all out here," Lambert said. "I'm part of her team. She's in charge." Technically true.

"Pissed off now. I shot her with a stun gun about ten minutes ago, and that didn't work. Her friends back at the casino have a sniper, so I suggest you keep your heads down and keep moving."

"Not a concern," Kaden said.

"Is she one of yours?"

Lambert snorted. "Dream on."

"I have my reasons for asking," Henderson said, "self-preservation being number one."

"Your Team Three must be fucking impressing someone if they sent him down here to meet you," Kaden told Lambert. "He's a warlord."

He went right to his poker face. "My team is aware. He's not the only one here, either." It might true enough.

"The Sixth are shooting at the Sixth. There are a handful of Nomads. What do you think Vance is up to?" Kaden asked. "Other than trying to get us to kill each other."

Chapter Ten

Outskirts of Platte River Center

Shannon skirted the riverbank, avoiding the sheets of ice beginning to break free. Muddy, damp, and cold. She didn't expect this to be the spring thaw, but a minor relief from winter. There was nothing to show their winters were less harsh than the ones in Montana.

A lone car raced up the road, and she crouched low, hidden in the underbrush. As she understood things, cars were commonplace here and along the interstate east, although the outlanders rarely used them for more than bothering the sentries. It didn't slow down as it passed. They were trying to spook her. Half a dozen riders had circled back out towards the east, recognizing what invisible line not to cross. In a few more minutes, they'd be following the river west of her to make another run past the sentries. It looked to her like a regular occurrence, that they tested each other's defenses and the resolve of the Peacekeepers. The Nomads in Montana annoyed Vista Security in a similar way.

She'd started off balance, having both her partners back in her sensory range after a long absence. True, she'd been seeking them, Wade because he was being an ass, rather than accepting help from them, but that was how he'd always operated. He wouldn't be aware Cody had been granted status as a separate entity from The Vista. He wouldn't know a lot of things; she hadn't either until she'd communicated with Mac, and the shock of Council and Command breaking with each other hadn't been unexpected. Wade pretended not to care, and it was a blatant lie he told.

"Come on, let's dance," she murmured impatiently. The Nomads appeared to be moving away, heading east. "I'm not walking miles out past my safe zone." Wade would be pissed, and he'd forbid it, still believing he got to boss her around. He didn't, not now. It wouldn't interfere with the plans they had set in motion.

They couldn't redo this either; they couldn't catch everyone by surprise again. Shan got onto the blacktop, remnants of the interstate, well preserved considering the harsh weather Nebraska had. Digging around in one of the many pockets of her parka, she found a flare gun.

~You better be ready~, she warned Wade. Then she fired the flare low over the road. Anyone close would be able to tell where it came from. Farther out, they could only guess.

Within minutes, three cars roared over the crest, two trying to run the third off the road. She watched from the bank, in cover, waiting them out. A hundred yards down the road, the rear car erupted in a ball of flames, debris flying off the road into the river.

"Lambert," Shan yelled, waving her hands in the air for a moment, knowing who had fired. He liked to blow things up. It meant the Vistans had converged on the casino, and that they identified who was Nomad and who was the Sixth.

A fourth car appeared, not handling the patchy ice as well, and careened out of control. Moments later, the one they'd been pursuing appeared from the access road and t-boned him. Glass shattered, and metal screamed from the impact. Then, silence. Both drivers emerged, and a brief gunfight ensued. The driver from the first car, faster or more accurate, and his opponent dropped.

Shan watched it all from where she stood, her own semi-autos drawn. She recognized him, even though it was about to be the first time they met.

"There are more hostiles coming up behind me, if you're interested," he called across the road. "Or we could get the hell out of here." Older than Hunter, and with something distinctly military about him.

"I don't jump into a car with every man that asks," she parried, adrenaline running. An imminent firefight was clouding her thoughts. That tunnel-vision she'd been warned about countless times.

"Suit yourself." He ducked back in, revved the engine and pulled a U-turn in the road. Then he backed up until he was beside her. The passenger-side window unrolled. "Get in the damned car, Capt. Allen. I'm not joking about a whole band of outlanders headed this way in a pissed-off mood."

Tucking her Sigs away, she crossed the road and let herself in the passenger side, rolling the window up.

"Seat belt. Otherwise, if you can hit a moving car with a shotgun, feel free to try."

".28 gauge," she suspected, examining the weapon in the rack attached to the dashboard.

"Yeah, Weatherby semi-auto."

"Great." She latched her seat belt on, popping the glove box open. Shells, a few far too large. "Who has an elephant gun?" Shan held up the brass 10-gauge shell.

"It's in the trunk. Sometimes they have armored vehicles."

"We have dozens of armored cars in a depot back home." In The Vista. That was some of the heavy equipment they maintained, just in case.

"I know you do," he whispered, glancing sideways at her. "I've watched you."

She spent a few moments analyzing him. It could have been a creepy stalker sort of statement. It wasn't.

"Why am I the only person alive who uses my real name?" Shan asked. Harlan was Yates, even if he was Harlan Yates and he was sitting right next to her.

"Because you started out on this little adventure trusting people too much." He punched it, flying down the interstate.

"I don't trust anyone, never have."

"Except Wade and MacKenzie."

"That's a gimme, Harlan." His driving didn't frighten her. Shan knew he had memorized the roads, and they'd be close to the Platte River Center, close enough to expect help.

"Okay, I'll re-phrase it. You put too much confidence in the integrity of the human race. Once upon a time, you believed people were trustworthy."

"People are trustworthy. Generally. Just not the sort of people we tend to cross paths with."

He nodded. "I can see you believe that."

"You don't?"

A car came into view behind them. "I think humanity is worth saving. It's not as easy as it sounds."

"You know it." She stifled a yawn.

"It's before noon," Harlan pointed out. "You should have thought about getting some rest last night, with the big day today." He was aware of what they were up to and wanted her to know the plans weren't so secret. It wasn't complicated.

"Keeping track of everyone eats energy. I don't want to shoot the wrong person, or jump in a car with the wrong person." She released her seat belt, grabbed the shotgun, and unrolled her window. Being young and limber, Shan sat on the edge of the window, pointing the shotgun at the car coming up behind them. The driver stood on his brakes and disappeared in a cloud of smoke and dust.

Settling back in her seat, she asked, "That doesn't happen to Kaden?"

"It does. I think he has better control."

"No shit," she offered. "I have more control of this car than my Gen En abilities."

"Hang on," he warned as the original car zoomed up on them from the access road and caught them in the rear quarter panel. Harlan kept it on the road. A black Humvee with metal plates welded over the side windows caught up, joining in the chase, and slammed into them harder and faster. This time, he lost control, and the car fishtailed. Then they were in the mud. When it spun over the embankment, it rolled right into the South Platte River.

She didn't have her seat belt on, and was bleeding from her head, dazed. The water was ice-cold and brought her around fast. They were upside down and at least partially submerged. "Shit, Harlan," she shouted, trying to push her door open with no luck.

"Don't," he warned. "Don't panic, we can get out."

"I can't swim."

"The water isn't deep."

"Fuck." She kicked at the door, and it didn't budge. She kicked it again.

"It's jammed against something." Then he grabbed her arm to get her attention. "Capt. Allen, snap out of it. We can get out and walk to shore. I'm not going to let you drown." Water started filling the car, and he knew the outlanders would be waiting. She'd realize that too if she kept her wits about her. "I was a Navy SEAL. I can swim for you and me and not break a sweat. Do not panic."

She nodded.

"Can you follow me? Are you hurt?"

"I'm not."

He swiped the blood from her face and showed it to her. She looked surprised. "Follow me out of the car. Be ready to come up shooting."

"Okay."

"Shannon, what's my name?" he asked, unsure if she was okay.

"Harlan Yates. You used to be a Navy SEAL. Before I was born."

"Ouch. You're fine. Let's go before we get hypothermia." He

rolled down his window, letting in a rush of water. They had a small bubble of air left moments later. "Take a deep breath and follow me. It's maybe ten feet."

Shan nodded, took a breath and dove after him.

———

"Do something," Hunter demanded, watching the scene unfold out across the interstate from the rooftop of the casino. "They went in the river, and it's at fucking flood stage."

"It's nowhere near flooding," Ueda scoffed. "They can get out."

"And get shot."

"Priority emergency," Wade spoke on his handset to appease him. "Lambert, Team Zero is out of commission, half-a-mile south of you. Disabled and in the South Platte River. They are not alone. Taylor One, back them up. Move your team. If Henderson runs, let him."

"Team Zero?" Hunter asked.

"Someone not us," Wade told him. "Meaning Harlan. Saying their names on the air would be incredibly bad right now."

"I'm going," Hunter said.

Wade knew he couldn't order him not to, and that Hunter would be more than glad to tell him so. "It will be over by the time you get out there."

"Fuck you," Hunter challenged him. "Because you sent her out there."

"I did. It's her job."

Hunter backed off, ready to bolt. "You're going to get her killed over something neither of you can control, and both of you think you can." He spun on his heels and disappeared down the stairwell.

"Tell your partner to let him take the car," Wade said.

Ueda nodded.

———

"Harlan is one of my oldest and best friends," Moore said, glad they had called him Henderson on the air. "Where are they?"

Lambert pointed, already moving, Kaden and Tero with him. It was too far in the mud and slush. "There are hostiles on the scene. Engage at will and be aware we have a secondary team moving in as well."

"We don't need your permission. If Harlan's there, he can handle it," Kaden said, more to reassure himself. Then he urged the horse into a gallop, following Lambert's lead.

"The idea is not to shoot any of my people," Lambert said.

"I got that," Kaden answered, giving a crystal-clear impression that he shouldn't push. "I'm aware of who belongs where. Tero won't shoot anyone unless he has no option."

"A pacifist?" Moore speculated.

"Through and through. I won't let harm come to our people, regardless," Tero said.

Lambert didn't want to know if he'd been in an actual firefight before. "If you can't, keep out of the way." There was gunfire ahead, shouting, then silence. Jumping off his horse, long rifle in hand, Lambert ran towards the chaos.

"Do what he said," Kaden ordered, grabbing his AK, and following him. "Watch behind us. They run in packs."

Moore waited with the younger men, not knowing who was enemy and who was ally. He recognized that he'd walked into the center of a firestorm. Even the warlords didn't have a simple fix for this. Nothing was ever easy.

Lambert flung himself onto the muddy ground, took careful aim with the big gun, and fired. He didn't look up or slow down as Kaden joined him.

The water was deeper than either of them had guessed, and once she cleared the car, Shan had a flashback to her childhood. She'd almost drowned in the pond behind their house, and water was the first thing she'd ever had a fear of. As she lost sight of Harlan in the muddy, icy water, she did what he'd told her not to do, and panicked. Her gear, water-resistant and close to forty pounds of it. She tried to kick for the surface and barely moved.

~Don't panic,~ Wade thought.

~Too late.~

Harlan hadn't lied about not leaving her. He grabbed the front of her parka and swam backwards. In two strokes he broke the surface, dragging her up beside him. In two more, she felt her feet hit solid ground. The cold put everything in slow motion.

Everything for them, not for the outlanders who had run them into the river. As the pair dragged themselves towards the bank, the Nomads opened fire from the road. Shan acted, and that defensive response, that moment of hesitation kicked in, making them all pause. One moment. She didn't know how to trigger it, but it happened. Once earlier at Henderson, and now, as they moved in for the kill. As they hesitated, Shan fired, angry that her reflexes responded at half-speed. The Nomads scattered.

"Where are they?" Harlan asked, knowing she could track them, at least for a short time. He'd seen Kaden do it often enough.

"About five seconds from a fight with our backup teams." She stumbled onto the bank, shivering. It wasn't shock; it was the cold.

Harlan wasn't too proud to admit he was hurt. "I hope they have a medic."

"They do." She felt the strength draining from her. She had been over-extending her abilities for days. Harlan got her arm over his shoulder, and they managed to make it up the embankment. Two outlanders lying next to the forward car, not going anywhere, quite dead.

Gunfire close made them both refocus.

"We've got to get out of the cold." He felt her legs buckle and got her to the pavement. It would be a few degrees warmer, but they needed more. Freezing to death was an imminent possibility.

Hunter spotted them, saw them both collapse, and ran. Lambert was clearing out the rest of the intruders, and Taylor One had to be close. She'd warned Hunter, once it started, they couldn't turn back. So far, two of their targets were acquired, Harlan and Henderson. One to go. "I need assistance," he called on his radio as he ran.

"Hypothermia," Harlan said as the younger man approached, and Shan didn't shoot him.

"I know," Hunter said. "If you can get moving, do it."

Shan interrupted, pushing herself up and checking her Sig. "West, incoming."

Both men turned to watch the road, weapons ready, knowing she wouldn't have alerted them if it was their people returning from the chase. An entire platoon of Peacekeepers marched into view, in full riot gear.

"Are they on our side?" Hunter asked. They stood by him.

"If they aren't," Shan told him, impressed with the display, "you'd better do some fast name-dropping."

DeTessa regarded the men, intrigued and amused. Alarmed too at what had happened without her knowledge. She more often than not had an inkling about matters involving the Platte River Center. As an Elder, she heard about things like this beforehand. The other ten Council Elders sitting in the hall were there to observe, having voted many years ago for her to be their voice. Later, they'd have an in-depth discussion of the events, along with the several absent. The only other people in the hall were several Peacekeepers, stoic as usual, and a handful of observers assisting the Elders.

"Lambert, Elliott, and Taylor, I know you," she spoke succinctly. Today, on an uninterrupted free day, she was dressed in formal red; a maroon ankle-length dress, adorned with gold and black embroidery, a matching scarf, and a bright red cord braided into her hair, holding it back. "Where are the younger Taylor and Cassie Elliott?"

Lambert took a step forward. "Elder Jardin, they are at our quarters. They weren't involved in this altercation."

"They're civilians," Taylor added.

"Civilians. Interesting word. It's also interesting that my Peacekeepers have brought us warlords this morning. That hasn't happened in years. You are more careful than whatever this was," she waved her hand dismissively.

Henderson nodded, "Yes, ma'am. We didn't mean to intrude, but events called for neutral ground."

"Neutral until you ride through here and try to kill each other."

"We didn't consider it would get out of hand."

She paced a few steps. A pause in front of Kaden, and a nod, indicating she knew who he was. "I don't know you," she spoke to Tero, "Or you." Hunter. "I might know you," she corrected. "I'll have to see about who you are."

Wade was up next. "A warlord by any other name."

"Yes, ma'am," he said.

"Here is the young lady from the infirmary."

A pair of sentries escorted Shannon forward. She'd been given dry clothes, and relieved of her weapons, for the time being.

DeTessa regarded her. "I don't know you. The man dragged out of the river with you, however, is yet another warlord. He's confined to the infirmary for now."

Sometimes, Shan recognized when to shut up.

DeTessa eyed the group. Muddy, cold, hurt, but not beaten, not at all. "Who is in charge of this rabble?" No one stepped forward. "Someone determined this was 'neutral ground', and that you should come here to fight among yourselves. Who was it?"

Shan and Wade exchanged turbulent looks for a moment, and Kaden snickered.

"None of this is funny," DeTessa chided him.

"You're right," Kaden apologized.

"Four men died out there today, and every one of you is quite lucky that none of them were my men or citizens of Platte River Center. Now, who wants to take responsibility for this?"

"What charges are we facing?" Wade asked.

"Charges? There are no charges. It happened outside the city, outside my jurisdiction, so you've broken none of our laws. The boundaries here are defined. The outlanders know this, too. You may have to deal with them at some point because of this. I merely want to understand who is responsible." She spoke with infinite patience.

"I am," Wade said.

"No," Shannon disagreed. "It was a group effort, and you are the least responsible for this because you've been hiding here in the south for weeks." Years, if she was realistic. He'd never really come home after his first run-in with Rafe.

"Shut up," Kaden told her.

"Warlord, we'll have words if necessary. This concerns you, but I want to hear from them first, from those called Team Three." She regarded them.

"Today has resulted from a year of planning," Wade didn't mind explaining. All three targets, the three people they needed to cement their place in Cody, and the safety of The Vista, had been acquired now. Jardin. He hoped she wouldn't take offense at being considered a target. There was no hostile intent.

"What is it you're here to do?"

"What we said. We're here because Platte River is neutral ground. There are people fighting over the trade routes, and some of those people would rather we not be involved, to the extent of having us killed. That's why it took us a year. That's why we had to get here on our own. As a team, we were moving targets."

"Do you understand why?" DeTessa asked, her voice softening.

"We do."

"I'd like to speak to you alone. Team Three, or the ones who are here now."

The rest of the Vistans looked unsure. "It's not a Security issue," Shan said.

"I don't want to leave you here," Hunter spoke up.

Shan grabbed his hand and leaned close to whisper. "It's easier this way. We're here to make a treaty that will force Vance to act."

"It's not that simple."

"We're aware of this. Go."

"Be careful."

She nodded. "We're in no danger here, I swear." He hesitated to join the others, but followed.

"Warlords, stay," DeTessa said. "This concerns you." She dismissed the rest of the crowd with a wave. The Peacekeeper who remained was her son, Marco. A pair of Elders also departed.

The Vistans wouldn't like being kicked out, but Shan had an eerie sense it was for the best. There were things they'd never speak of, not to their friends, not to family, Council, or Command. Things that were better forgotten.

"A bit possessive, is he?" DeTessa asked, amusement in her eyes.

"Not at all. Worried. We've had difficulties getting here."

"Haven't we all?" A shadow of sadness crossed her face. "Later, when we've made our peace with one another, we should talk again. First, we're here to discuss why you're here. My initial impression was to have you all thrown in confinement to cool off for a few days."

Each of them wore different expressions of shock or dismay.

DeTessa laughed, a genuine, warm sound. "You'd have considered the same thing. To answer one question, you're easier to find when you're together, because you amplify one another's abilities." She eyed Wade. "You lead them."

"I lead Team Three."

"To help hide your friends from what?"

"From the past," Wade said. "The Altered were exterminated. We know that now."

"What you perceive is a sliver of the truth."

"We understand that too, Elder Jardin. We want to understand."

"Are you so certain?"

"Yes, we are," Wade spoke for the team, even if Mac was absent.

"After the turn of the millennium, the Altered were never meant to live alongside humans. We were meant to replace the majority of the population, in considerably smaller numbers. We were meant to be controlled. The process was already happening when war broke out and put a stop to their schemes. The Altered were evolving by then. Inevitably, they would fail in controlling us."

"We weren't meant to replace everyone," Shannon went on, having heard the story from the warlord standing next to her.

"The elite and powerful planned to use us for whatever means they needed. There were thousands of influential families, funding, legislating, and hiding the Altered, at the end. They assumed they owned us. Unlike people after the war, they didn't mind if their bloodlines crossed. In fact, it was encouraged." DeTessa thought about something. "The Altered weren't chosen at random, after all. They wanted us to be strong, intelligent, and adaptive. What they didn't anticipate was that our abilities would change without prompting, and erratically."

"We're not the Sixth," Wade said.

"What do you think the Sixth are?"

"Altered that resulted from the more experimental procedures towards the end."

DeTessa clasped her hands behind her back. "Who told you this fairy tale?" she asked. She already knew, but she asked anyway.

Shan looked at Kaden.

"Warlord, what name are you going by now?"

"Kaden Yates, Elder Jardin."

Wade and Shan exchanged looks for a moment.

"Harlan Yates is your father."

"I was adopted, but yes."

"Wildblood," Shan threw the word out for them.

"A Wildblood is an untrained Altered," Kaden said.

"A Wildblood is an aware Altered, not subject to the training corporations forced on those they deemed their property," DeTessa corrected. "By training, I refer to brainwashing and what can only be considered torture in a polite, civilized society."

"I concur," Kaden said.

"Enlighten us as to the nature of your biological parents, if you would."

"I only know what Harlan told me, but I have no reason to doubt him. What you're looking for is a simple statement. Both of my biological parents were Altered."

Shannon resisted the urge to look at Wade again. He'd been right about offspring and genetics all along.

"A brief, truncated version of the history of the Sixth. The Sixth Consortium was a biotech lab that originated near Washington, DC, former capital of the former United States of America, capital of the Allied States of New England. It had facilities in numerous countries, including Brazil. They were the first corporation that allowed altered humans to procreate. It is believed that the abilities labeled 'psychic' were derived from the synesthesia experiments they began in the 1960s. All Altered correctly identified as 'The Sixth' are progeny of these; a small percentage exhibit abilities that are not classified in any manner because there is no accurate name for them."

"A Sixth would have Altered parents," Wade repeated for clarity.

"Yes," DeTessa surmised for them. "At least one, occasionally both. A Sixth can be a Wildblood, but not all Wildblood are the Sixth. Not all the Altered developed psychic abilities, and the ones that did are always connected to the original Altered the Consortium developed. Then the war changed everything."

"I thought the purpose of the Altered project was to improve us as a race. What happened?"

"The blood knows blood. The changes aren't always good and noble, and the talents aren't always passed on, but other traits are. Some bloodlines are more familiar than others, and that is why some of us perceive who we are without asking. It's not a mystical thing; it's pure science. Now, a lost science. What happened was human greed and hubris."

Putting a hand up, Shan steadied herself on Kaden's shoulder, closing her eyes for a moment. For clarity.

"Capt. Allen, you don't look so good," DeTessa observed.

"Rough day," Shan replied, straightening, looking right back at her. "I heal fast, but it's been a rough day." She was pale.

"It has been a day, hasn't it? I think we shall continue this conversation at a later date. Yates should be able to join us by then, as well. The Peacekeepers outside will show you to your rooms," DeTessa dismissed them.

"Are we being detained?" Wade repeated his first concern.

"No. You can meet with your people at leisure. I've had all of you moved to the cul-de-sac across the plaza, where your accommodations will be attended to. Do you need to return to the infirmary, young lady?"

"I need to rest; I don't care where."

"I'd like all my people in the same vicinity," Wade said. "We have medics."

"I have an aide on the premises for you, in case you require assistance."

Once outside, Shan confronted her partner. "We need to talk."

"Nothing has changed. I'm here to negotiate with Elder Jardin. You've got Harlan; Lambert has Henderson. None of us had met each other before today, and we have specific goals. We can't change our intent, especially not now."

"I hadn't planned to."

"You really do look pitiful."

"I hurt everywhere, I'm still cold, and I need to sleep. Please, please tell Mac what is happening here. We have to keep in contact."

"I'll take care of it," he promised. "Hunter and I had words."

"When?" Shan groaned.

"About half a second after you went into the river."

She shivered, remembering the water filling the car, and the sensation she couldn't escape. "I'll talk to him."

"No need. If we have a brawl, we have a brawl; it won't be the first. He has your best interests in mind, but he's uncertain whether he's helping or hindering you. He worries he might be putting you in more danger."

"That's what he thinks?"

"I thought you should be aware. If you trust him, so do I. There's one more thing I got crystal clear from the few minutes with him on that rooftop."

"Sure there was."

"He's insecure."

"We've had long discussions about Mac..."

"Not Mac," Wade told her. He'd seen something else. "Because he's not Altered."

"No shit." Shan rubbed her eyes.

"One step at a time. Talk to Hunter, and reassure him this is only business. Get that treaty with Black Hills. Once we're done here, we move on to the next step."

"Are we a team again?"

"Still. I won't apologize for what I did."

"Is the next step going home, or to Estes Park?"

"All this is going to get the attention of Skolkovo. We see they aren't on good terms with any of us. Maybe we can encourage them to step in concerning Vance. If not, it'll be time to make a new plan. I don't know what, but Vance isn't invincible."

Chapter Eleven

Platte River Center noon March 5

Mitch and Cassie sat on the floor towards the front of the auditorium, playing cards and watching Shan and Chris pretend to spar with each other. It had snowed, and the entire city came to a standstill, at least for a few days. They were used to the winter, the snow, the boredom, and the need to keep themselves occupied. The unfamiliarity of the place was making them all a little edgy. Taylor One had disappeared on different errands. The others had gone to the gym to work out their frustration over yet another delay.

The latter pair had found foam boxing gloves and were pretending to fight. Chris was perplexed, bouncing between wanting to show them he could defend himself, and not wanting to take a swing at Shan.

"She's going to punch you right in the nose," Mitch warned, knowing this from experience.

"I thought this was practice."

"When you practice at the shooting range, you use bullets, don't you?"

Shan grinned, letting him guess. She dodged around the floor, fluid, fast, and less interested in the boxing match than the guests joining them. Harlan wandered in, his left arm in a sling, Kaden close on his heels.

"I've seen her beat up Green, and he's the one who taught her to fight," Mitch said.

"Maybe Green won't hit a woman," Cassie offered.

"Sure he will," Shan said. "He's hit me. Hell, he's knocked me down half a dozen times until I kept my hands up and stopped giving him a tell when I was about to take a swing."

"Ouch," Cassie said. "Full-on punches, or this play stuff?"

"Green has no problem, male or female, if he's training you." She dodged away from Chris. He'd already decided he wasn't going to hit her. No way, no how.

"You give as good as you get, if I remember," Mitch said.

"Yeah, now, after a few years. Besides, Green likes it when I smack him."

Chris dropped his hands. "Come on. Information I don't need to hear."

"And that would earn you a nice black eye," she told him, relaxing her stance. Game over. "If you can shock or surprise your opponent, even for a second, it might give you the advantage you need. Everything is fair in a fight. I've shown you that trick before."

Chris looked disgusted, dropping the gloves and returning to the brunch they'd brought along. Pancakes topped with dried fruit and sweet cream. Platte River seemed to have a decent stockpile of goods, and they were guests, at least for now. Wade would meet with DeTessa soon. None of them would be aware of when. Same with Lambert and Henderson. Shan's meeting was less discrete for a reason.

"You should tell me about that sometime," Cassie grinned.

Dropping her gloves, Shan went to greet the pair. "They let you out."

"To get some fresh air," Harlan said. "When they said 'fresh air', I didn't know there was a couple feet of snow on the ground."

"He doesn't heal like you do," Kaden reminded her.

"I had a vest on," Shan said.

"I've been informed you're here to talk about a treaty, and I'm the lucky man getting to negotiate," Harlan said.

"More of an order than an invitation for me."

"Let's talk, then," he offered. "Alone as long as you're comfortable." They wandered away to one of the empty alcoves along the north side of the building.

"You did just hear that conversation?"

"Do you think you could take me, or Kaden?"

"I have several advantages in a fight, and several disadvantages."

"Surprise, sure, but I learned that trick a long time ago. I meant on even terms."

"There are no even terms. I'm Gen En, and there's no way to turn that off."

"One of those Wildblood things."

She peered at him. "You saw one of those things when we came out of the river. The Nomads seemed startled for a moment and froze. I did that. No, I don't control the effect. It happens when I'm in a confrontation, but not every time. Also, we're not fond of that term."

"Capt. Allen, what would you prefer I call you? Capt. Allen is tedious and impersonal." Charming. Part of the reason Shan would be the one to work with him, an idea Vance had put out there before they became aware of the fact they were not allies. Harlan appreciated a pretty woman, one of those minor advantages.

"Shannon is fine. Wildblood is a thing, I'm a person, and I'm trying to be counterproductive to what they wanted from us."

"That I believe."

"I've said things you don't believe?" They found a sunny window, complete with a table and chairs, near the kitchen, across the building, giving them a bit of privacy. The Vistans and Kaden were already involved in another discussion.

Harlan took a seat opposite her. "I know you better than you imagine. Your team, some of your more interesting habits, and other things. By no means everything."

"You watched us with Kaden's help, and all that information is outdated by two years."

"We've watched you. Kaden had nothing to do with it until recently, for a variety of reasons. The most obvious being that he wasn't up north."

"He was in Colorado, causing problems for Rafe."

"That's not accurate either," he told her. "There are other Altered. I'm certain you've taken that into account. Black Hills has an extensive network of people, there and abroad."

"Including in The Vista."

He smiled and inclined his head a bit, not denying the accusation. No point. She was as intriguing as Kaden claimed, in a Wildblood way. "I'm not at liberty to discuss my team members."

"Taylor brought Kaden to my house not too many months ago."

"Discreet."

"A group of us in Security grew up together. We share some habits, even some habits that might be mistaken for Altered habits. Discretion isn't one."

"So why are we here?"

"Our conversation stays between us. Convince me."

"I can swear to you, give you my word, whatever you'd like. You'll either accept that or not."

She was satisfied with that. "Team Three vets our potential allies, although others have taken on the task. It doesn't mean we've changed the rules; it means we've adapted."

"That makes you dangerous," Harlan said.

"We were dangerous before. Vance tried to use us. I suppose he did in a way. Rafe is gone." She drummed her fingers on the table. "As I understand it, you were with them for a time."

"We traveled together. It was never as cozy as you and your fellow Vistans."

Shan kept a rude remark to herself. The personality conflicts in the teams were apparent. One reason they'd made their way to Platte River in groups. Fewer issues, at least until they added outsiders to the mix.

"Two years ago, Vance let Rafe act on his idea to eliminate us. Why then?"

"Rumor has it, he thought you had turned the tables on him. You traveled into Colorado, and they both assumed the worst."

"We didn't know either of them was there until Rafe tried to kill us. Then Wade went after him. None of us had plans to expand anywhere other than Cody. Now Wade wants to go as far as he can, as fast as he can."

"Is that why the sudden interest in the Sixth, the warlords, and Black Hills?"

"The safety net will benefit both cities. You convinced Mac. So would a trade agreement. Trade routes. My job is to convince you."

"Let's talk about what The Vista needs, and what Black Hills needs. Let's talk about the problems we're going to face, because I guarantee you, Vance has people here to find out what we're doing."

"We are aware. I can only speak for Team Three and Cody Security," Shan told him, getting comfortable. "Later, that will change, but The Vista ruling bodies and I aren't on good terms."

"I represent the Black Hills Council."

"You're a warlord."

"I am, but I don't speak for other warlords in this matter."

Several people had congregated in the Auditorium, the Vistans mingling with them. Shan didn't feel comfortable with the idea, but she wasn't in charge of anything at the moment.

"They throw a dance here every weekend. I'm sure The Vista has dances. You know, socializing involving music, and fun."

"I know what a dance is."

"You shy away from public engagements, from socializing. It's a common trait of the Altered."

She ignored the statement, but he was correct. "I haven't been told how far along Cody and Black Hills are concerning an arrangement to build the security net. This meeting took planning, but some finer points weren't a concern until we arrived here."

"Cmdr. MacKenzie and I have gotten to basics. We've done an exchange for training. My people in security, and his concerning the electronics involved with the net. Other things too, things I suspect you'd find boring. A master gardener came out for a few weeks to see how we manage our growing season. We've had caravans running when the weather permits. They did an aerial survey of the city for us."

"We need to figure out a time frame for the construction. Unless Mac gets those caches supplied, winter is going to shut us down hard. The first hundred and fifty miles, from Cody to Big Timber, are harsh. Driving it is bad in the summer, impossible in the winter."

"There were caches and camps in the planning stages. He started before the snow. In case you didn't notice, we're still in winter; a couple of months of decent weather to work on this." Harlan didn't disguise the smile at her. "You've got a tight-knit core group, Shannon. You're lucky."

"Not so lucky. We've lost people on this little adventure."

"What happened in December to cause the shift away from The Vista?"

"I'm not at liberty to say," the blank response returned.

He nodded. "Vance is still hitting you."

Shan didn't answer. Knowing about The Vista's internal problems wasn't something she felt necessary to reveal. If Vance was being a problem, it was being withheld from the people at Cody.

"This is one of those things we're supposed to be planning to help one another with. I learned his tactics. Since Rafe is gone, he's lost his chief enforcer, and he's concerned Skolkovo will step in. If they do, he'll lose Estes Park, and that puts us in a good position."

"Good for you, bad for the Front Range, bad for Angelfire."

"Good for us," he elaborated, "because that would hand us some trade routes Angelfire can't hold. Too bad for Angelfire."

"You don't want Skolkovo extending itself."

"Everything we've heard about Caulder and his city is conjecture. He doesn't like the Altered. Hell, it would be a toss-up between who he hated more, the Russian or the Altered."

At the mention of Angelfire, Kaden made his way across the floor to join them.

"I'm here to negotiate with Harlan," Shan told him. "I can't discuss this with you."

"Why?"

"They did not specify."

"They?"

"Come on, Kaden," Shan rubbed her eyes. "You were there that night; you saw what Command did. So now, I mean Team Three. We decide what we are going to do. I can't tell you. I decided, for a lot of reasons. The most important being, no one knows everything."

"Then tell him about Angelfire."

"I thought you would have."

"Our conversations are between you and me," Kaden deflected. "If I were to guess, I'd say you left there to come here."

"What does The Vista need?" Harlan asked. Angelfire was a discussion for another time.

She was aware they were tag-teaming her. "We've been sitting in that valley since the war. It's stagnating. We need to expand, to see what's in the world, even if we don't like what we find. Even if it's dangerous. Cody is the first step. Once upon a time, we were content with that. We may scatter to the wind."

"You and Wade?"

"Wade certainly. I'd like to. People in Cody, and even The Vista, are free to make their own decisions. I don't see many of the original survivors being interested. They're happy, they're safe."

"But you're curious," Harlan finished for her.

"We recognized there was an entire world out here. We knew we couldn't be the only ones. And we were aware someone was watching us."

"You were right," Kaden added. "But do you know who was watching?"

She considered it, looking at Kaden. Not only him, but she couldn't pinpoint who else. "I have an idea."

He nodded. "You're here, and you'll find out." With that, he wandered away towards a group of young women gathering near the meal line.

"And they call me dramatic," Shan said, eliciting a smile from Harlan. "To answer your question, yes. Vance is still our primary concern."

"I've set up a trade agreement between Cody, Black Hills, and pretty soon The Vista, if Cmdr. MacKenzie is correct. There has to be a reason, a specific one if I understand the Altered as well as I do."

"Trust. I could have done without going in the river to find out how far I can trust you."

"I could have done without that too." He patted his arm. "Lucky it was a ricochet."

"You win."

"It's not a competition, Shannon. I've got nothing to hide, and you can pry it out, if I did."

"Is that an offer?"

"It is. I realize you can see my thoughts."

"Not exactly, and not without effort."

"Kaden has told me it's not a thing to be explained."

Shan leaned back, taking a deep breath. "Last chance to say nevermind."

"Nothing to hide." He understood, a dangerous claim to make.

"Sure. None of us do. You tell people Kaden is your son, and they assume, biological," she started off. "That's what you want, too. People don't know the semantics of the Altered. Hell, I don't. You let them think it, though, because they don't associate one with the other. The Altered didn't come from families. They came from sterile biotech laboratories. As long as they believe that, you hope you can worry a little less about him."

"Easy enough to figure out."

She continued. "Okay, then. When you meet new people, the first thought in your mind isn't one of trust. Usually, you wonder if you'll have to kill any of them, and then you single out who is in charge. Just in case. You couldn't decide between Mac and Ballentyne, back in Cody."

Harlan didn't have an immediate answer. She'd read him, like Kaden warned. One of his darkest fears, too. That worried him. Their first encounter beyond The Vista had been with Rafe, and it warped their views.

"Now that I've dredged that up to give you nightmares, I'll tell you one of mine."

"You don't need to do that," he whispered.

"Yes, I do. We don't like to intrude like that, so it's only fair to share."

"I understand. No harm, no foul."

"You saw something rare. I panicked; nothing fake about it. I can't swim, and upside down in a sinking car, I can't imagine a worse scenario." She blinked, shaking it off. "It's not that I've never rolled a car, because I have. It was the water, and it was so damned cold, I could barely move."

"Fear of water is a common phobia. I love swimming, but I grew up on the beach."

"Wade does, too. That led to my fear of the water. The boys got me to jump into a pond when I was little, thinking they could teach me to swim because our parents never seemed to have the time. I almost drowned."

"I understand. Our trust issues are not unfounded. Sooner or later you'll realize there are a lot of good people out in the world, too."

"A couple of days ago you were trying to convince me that people are untrustworthy."

"I like to understand the motives of the people I work with. If you had no hope for us as a species, what would your motives be?"

"You asked what The Vista needs. The reason for the security net, the reason we are so careful when we confide in others. You've heard of our mantra, that no one knows everything."

"Good idea, good tactics," Harlan gave them that much.

"The point is, what I'm going to tell you is one reason The Vista has been kept isolated. It's not something you think you know."

"I was under the impression that no one believed there was anything left."

"That's what they tell us when we're children. This time, 'they' means the Council and Command, and anyone that's ever been a member of either. It wasn't just fairy tales. They made us believe it; they had proof. The videos of the war, the plague. For a lot of years, we fell for it."

"What changed your mind? Or what made you doubt the stories?"

"It wasn't one thing; it was a lot of little things that didn't add up right until they did. When Wade and I figured out I could see other Gen Ens, we did a survey. I've always told him how many, never who."

"How many?"

"A hundred and twenty-seven."

"Counting you?" Harlan teased.

"Counting us," she smiled. "That was the first time, and it took a couple of years to meet everyone. About three percent of our population."

"Concurrent with other statistics we've seen."

"Then I did it again a year ago."

"Are you going to make me guess?" he asked when she paused.

Shan crossed her arms and raised her eyebrows. "Give it a shot."

"The numbers changed."

"Yeah, they changed. Significantly."

"A change in the population?"

"No, not in the population, in me, after I'd been away."

"Maybe something was keeping you from seeing the others. Or someone."

"That's what I guessed. No one has confessed."

It took him a moment to realize it was joking. Seeing she had relaxed, even a little enough to make a joke, made him tense. If he identified one thing about Team Three, it was that they were always working on a plan. Always. "Why are you telling me this? I have a sneaking suspicion it's more than a treaty you have in mind."

"Team Three needs a point of retreat. We need a place not associated with us or The Vista, if the time comes when we have to run. Cody was that place until we established a base there."

Harlan shook his head. "A world where the children have to hide from those that came before them, the people that made them different. It's a fucked-up thing. How long have you been hiding?"

"Since we realized we weren't like most others. Wade was fourteen when he mapped out our first hideaway. All of us were sixteen when we joined Security, but our training started a couple of years before."

"You include MacKenzie whenever you talk about the team."

"Of course. Mac was the first member of Team Three. We all grew up in the same house. He convinced Wade to join. It seemed like a good way to hide some things we needed to hide."

"No one was suspicious of kids jumping into Security before they finished school?"

"Not at all. We were taught a lot of things in school that wouldn't have been dreamt of by our parents. Survival skills. Other skills as we got a little older and had an interest. By fourteen, most of us had an idea of what we were going to do for a career."

Harlan waited as a group passed by, heading outside. "What's in it for me, for Black Hills?"

"Want to learn about Angelfire? I'll give you the ten-minute tour and introduce you to the Senator."

"How did you manage that?"

"Long and complicated story. Short version, I have an ace."

"You're not going to tell me about it either."

"Not today. Other people are involved."

"I'd love to play cards with you. So, what's the next step?" He fidgeted, arm aching, pain relief wearing thin.

"As Team Three gathers the information we need here, we'll break off into splinter groups. Like how we got here. We'll have separate destinations."

"Ours will be Angelfire?"

"We haven't decided. I didn't get the chance to thank you either, for dragging me out of the river," she said.

"It's what I was trained to do, a lot of years ago. Old habits. Besides, it was a mutual effort."

"Fair enough. If you hear things, keep in mind that not all of them will be true. We've used the tactic of disinformation before."

"When you trust me more, you'll tell me."

"I can imagine," Shan said, curious. He liked to play mind games. Kaden had apparently picked up the habit from him.

"I've met your partners. Both say you're the smartest on the team."

Shan snorted, getting glances from across the room. "Are you going to tell me what you think you know about us?"

"When it's relevant, we'll talk." Harlan didn't see any point at the moment.

"You don't consider it is now? We're vulnerable here. If it weren't winter, we'd already be packing it up to move on again."

"There are a lot of players in motion. Give it a little time to slow down. We need to take a rest. With as many people as you have here, consider that the warlords have brought their own entourages along."

"We have people scattered over six states. More than four thousand civilians to protect. You might stop and remember I'm here to answer your questions."

"Ah, Shannon," he sighed, stretching. "In all seriousness, no. This isn't political jousting. I was told that when Rafe went after you, he killed the Altered he was there for."

Shan sat back in her chair, running the events of two years ago through her mind. "Were you told 'Team Three' or something else? Outlanders?" There had been other people involved, but no Vistans had died.

"An Altered, one he watched."

"That's wrong." Wade had been the target; Rafe had told her so himself.

"Meaning what?"

"They were misleading you or mistaken," she stated.

"I disagree. My source is good."

"I was there." She understood he saw her as the one lying about the ambush.

"Then we have a conundrum."

She didn't want to involve Kaden. He might see Mac for what he was. "We have to figure this out. Without trust, there is nothing."

Shan sank into the hot water, closing her eyes for a few minutes. Their room was dark and quiet, the faint scent of burning cedar in the fireplace. She leaned back against Hunter, relaxing. The chair pulled up next to the bathtub held two holstered handguns, a fifth of whiskey, and two cold glasses containing copious amounts of the amber liquid. Clean towels were draped over the back. After weeks of traveling across the frozen plains, a luxury retreat, albeit temporary.

"All good," Hunter whispered.

"Oh yes. Very good."

"This is it, isn't it? What you've been looking for all your life. Answers."

"I hope so. Ask me what you need to, because soon the warlords are going to come for us. Could be all of us."

"What do you mean, come for you?"

"The reason we're here. Make peace with them if we can. Figure out where we stand at least."

"Is this as dangerous as everything else we've done?"

"More than my usual day? No, I don't expect so. They've had plenty of opportunities to move on us, if that was their intent."

"Uh-huh. What are they going to tell you that will change your life?"

"Nothing, Hunter, nothing at all. We have all the cards, but we need to put them in the right order. That's what will come from this."

"This is going to make the split with Council a permanent thing."

"I think it already is. All this time, Command has been trying to cover for us, to keep us hidden, and we didn't understand. We were too close. Council has wanted control over Security from the beginning. It put Team Three in direct conflict with them."

"That's why Cody is so important."

She nodded.

"What do you plan on doing after the war?"

"What war?"

He laughed. "A metaphor, Captain. I've been right by your side for two years, through all of this. I followed you to Colorado; we came here together. We've lost friends."

"And found family."

"The point is, you've grown on me, and I like what we've got. It's not perfect, and I don't care. What are your plans when we're done here?"

"Plans. This has consumed us for so long."

"I said, what are your plans? Shannon, can you even consider anything as a single person, rather than as part of Team Three?"

"I don't think about it much." She was trying to skirt the issue, and they both knew it.

"It could be time to start."

"When we're alone, like now, it's just you and me. It would be pretty awkward otherwise," she laughed, having a long swig of whiskey.

"I know. The question still stands."

"Without considering anyone else, I have no idea."

"Come live with me."

"Where?"

"West, south, anywhere. Does it matter?" he asked. "Let's run away, and have our own lives."

She was quiet for a long time, finishing her drink. Hunter reached past her and turned on the water to reheat their bath.

"So," he said finally. "That means no."

"It means, maybe. You realize better than most, I come with attachments. Two of them."

"I am aware."

"I want to say something. It's not something I say often, or easily."

"Go on," he said.

She did. "I trust you, Hunter, and I love you. I can't make promises, but I like how it sounds. It can't be a permanent thing, because neither of us is capable of just quitting, and I'm part of Team Three."

"You're right," he conceded.

"A vacation. Have our own lives for a few weeks. Disappear for a while. Make a normal life, even if it's part-time."

"I can live with that."

Chapter Twelve

Platte River midday March 7

They strolled along the riverwalk, taking in the fresh air and clear skies. Wade entwined arms with DeTessa, making polite conversation. The serious words would come soon enough. A few steps behind them, Marco and Shannon kept pace, in full tactical gear, exchanging only nods. None of the residents going about their day gave them a second glance.

"You earned their loyalty," DeTessa observed in her usual elegant style. "I see that. Anyone who spoke to you in more than passing could."

"They're good people," Wade said. "Despite what you might hear."

"I believe you. You tell me your first concern is the safety of your home, and I trust that as well. How can we help each other?"

"A treaty of course, with The Vista. Trade next. I can offer you advice on what the Council Members will or won't agree to, but one thing we never wanted, to make enemies. And we have done that."

"You never had a choice in the matter," she assured him. "As for trade, you're aware there are standing agreements with Angelfire and Estes Park. Once upon a time, albeit a brief time, the warlords got along with each other and worked to keep what little civilization there was left. It's the reason the city is here." She patted his arm thoughtfully. "I don't want it to be a shock when you learn another of our allies, a territory we have treaties with for some years, is Skolkovo."

Wade took it all in, nodding. It wasn't a complete surprise.

"Skolkovo had a trade agreement with us long before Estes Park. That acquisition happened more recently."

"I spent several weeks there. Vance has a tight grip."

"Not so much this past year," she said, meaning Rafe wasn't there to enforce Vance's laws, and meaning she knew he was one of those responsible. She wouldn't speak it, but she knew.

So did he. "Yes, ma'am," Wade nodded.

"Is Capt. Allen hearing our conversation?"

"No, she's not. I'd say so if that were the case."

"I don't mind if she does, or you can tell her later."

"As long as I have your permission. You said we never had a choice in the enemies we made. I disagree."

"Even if you'd stayed in your home, never ventured south, never showed the ambition to find other people out here, he wouldn't let you be. At some point, for his own reasons, he'd have forced you to act."

"Are we talking about Rafe or Vance?"

"They were closer to being partners than you might believe from listening to Vance. They had a mutual ambition, and Vance gave him direction."

"We've heard," Wade said. "We've been told they wanted to invade The Vista while we were still young. Whose idea was that?"

"Unless you ask Vance and choose to believe him, there's no chance of knowing. I'd say the idea was mutual, and that they didn't act, understanding how it would end."

"How could they?"

"By the time you became an issue, The Vista was organized, defensive and well on the way to self-sustaining. Even then, you outnumbered any force they gathered by tenfold. It would have been a pointless fight. Most of their conscripts were farmers. Why do you think they waited for you to leave?"

Stopping along the walkway, Wade watched a dozen kids along the far bank, fishing and playing in the sun. "How did you learn these details?"

Out of earshot, their bodyguards paused, waiting. Marco, the tallest of the four; DeTessa not much shorter than Wade. It was an unusual crowd, with Shan being the shortest person. Wade caught that's what she considered as they stood there.

"Many of the Altered were trained to be solitary, antisocial creatures. Being forced into a situation that required interaction with many others, Altered and human, made conflict a daily ritual." DeTessa looked him in the eye. "We cut our own numbers in half before we broke and scattered."

"You were with them."

DeTessa let a wistful smile cross her face for a moment.

"You're a warlord," Wade said.

"Yes, I am, Cmdr. Wade. Quite a few people here know that; quite a few more don't understand the implications. There's no need to educate them. We are striving for the same goals, but as it is with you, some things are better left unsaid."

"I understand. Your words are safe with me." And he understood the sadness in her smile. "When Rafe started testing our defenses, were you aware?"

"Recently, you mean? We identified that he had moved from his usual enclave. With Vance's consent, of course. We inquired when we got word he was out of Colorado. We were told, 'Governor Vance is not his keeper, and Rafe is free to come and go as he wishes.' Later, of course, we learned of the results."

"What did Estes Park claim happened?" They continued on their walk.

"Concerning Rafe, nothing. A year ago we received a statement about losing communications with one of their camps earlier, and not being able to re-establish."

"I remember when I was small, The Vista had a crew that scanned the airways for years after the war, listening, waiting. A few people found their way to us, but it was a futile effort."

"Do you remember when they stopped?" DeTessa asked.

"I do. The summer, 2044, right after I turned ten," Wade reminisced. "I had no concerns about those things then, but I remember. We had a new Council; they had new ideas, better ideas on how to run things."

"They had new ideas. Not all of them were their own."

"Meaning what?"

"In the months previous, your Council made contact with those of us who would come to be called the warlords. Those of us not following Vance and Rafe. We gave them fair warning of our former colleagues' intent. That was a potent factor in the sudden silence and the change of your security protocols."

The flood of information Wade was processing threaded back to Shannon. She offered no response, physical reaction, or otherwise. Later, she would have an opinion; she always did. It was part of her job. Mac in Cody was aware as well.

"Why are you telling me this now?" Wade asked.

"Because we both realize the chances of Vance letting this go, of letting you and your team move beyond his range of influence, are slim. That stunt you pulled last week was a test of our defenses."

"The enemy of my enemy is my friend."

She peered at him. "That would be a fatal flaw in your reasoning, Cmdr. Wade. The greatest enemy you've had is the unknown. You knew so little when you wandered away from Montana, it nearly killed you. If you'd given them the chance, your own Command would have answered the questions they could."

"We have the problem of our governing bodies, the City Council and Security Command, not seeing eye-to-eye on issues. One of those issues being us."

"It's not an easy thing, trying to make all the decisions for your people. You're not going to be at peace with all of those decisions, and sometimes, you'll regret them. Don't let that stop you from trying."

"Why are you offering to help us?"

"Because we can. Some of us have the burden of protecting the rest of us. If I can make your journey a little less harsh, it will make my journey a little less harsh."

Wade nodded.

"If you stay here, it won't stop Vance. He'll bring his war here."

"How much time do we have?"

"You should ask what he will do when he acts."

"We didn't think he'd move on a neutral city, one he has trade interests in."

"He doubtless would. We won't force you to leave. The call is yours, and the consequences will be as well. Don't mistake my compassion for weakness."

"Never in my lifetime."

The usual crowd of people was on the streets after dark. A shift change at the mills that ran in the winter, and the dance had lasted late; routine safety patrols, and people enjoying the mild evening.

Wade and Shan watched from the second-floor deck of their complex, Lambert joining them. A terracotta chimenea was lit, helping stave off the cold, but it was March. They were bundled up, even being used to the cold. Inside, the rest of the Vistans waited, playing cards and watching a television they'd found in the downstairs library.

"She called you a warlord," Shan pointed out.

"She did. I've met a handful; we've had good words, and bad.

DeTessa said, 'by any other name'. I supposed she means, we're the same. Maybe literally, or maybe because I do the dirty work others don't want to consider."

"Stop pretending you're the only one," Lambert said. They had all started drinking earlier, and he was ready to argue.

"I never said I was. We've all done things we'll have nightmares about, and might always regret. A few years ago, I'd have blamed it on being Gen En. Now, I think it's how life is for everyone."

"Sure thing."

"Can you imagine what Command has gone through trying to keep us in line?" Shan cut in, an attempt to keep a fight from breaking out. "Hiding it from Council, all the time knowing they were lying about what was out here."

"We knew what we were getting into," Wade said, aware his mood was far from good. "Maybe more than we'd care to admit. This is bigger than us. We need the trade routes. If anyone knows how extensive civilization is, it'll be DeTessa."

"If we start fighting with each other, we might as well pack up, go home, and accept whatever happens," she said, her own anger still there. No one made her mad faster than Wade; not Hunter, not even Mac.

"Ouch," Lambert said. "It's been a long week, and none of us has slept worth a damn."

They paused, letting the tension in the air settle. Music drifted in from across the street, something lively and upbeat. A barbecue was happening at the park next to the river bend, and the scent of cooking food was on the breeze. The night was quite in the landscape beyond the lights of the city.

"I keep being told not every out here is looking for us. Not everyone has bad intentions." Shan let it go at that.

After a minute or two, Wade went on. "Henderson can tell us about the warlords, and where they fit in all this."

"Harlan has been helping work on the grid expansion since last autumn. The treaty needs to be settled, but it looks like you got the easier job this time."

"I don't think it's as simple as that," Wade said.

"You never do."

"And then, it's usually not."

"True," Lambert conceded. "What are your concerns? I'd be open to a trade-off."

Shan wrinkled her nose, considering it. "That might be all well and good, but Henderson tried to shoot me a few days ago."

"It was a Taser, and he was trying to keep you from getting killed by the outlanders we drew in. His fault, not his fault." Wade shrugged.

"He's lucky he's fast. When I shoot back, I'm not very forgiving."

"That's a 'no'," Lambert said.

"We're not making drastic changes now, not unless there is a genuine concern," Wade said. "If Black Hills has an issue they haven't disclosed, they'll tell us when they're ready, or when one of us sees it."

"So when are we going to talk about The Vista?" Shan asked.

"Whenever you're ready," Lambert answered too fast.

"Would it have made any difference if he had stayed?"

"No. Council would still have exiled the team, and Command would still have told them it wasn't in their jurisdiction. They'd still be fighting over it."

"I need to protect everyone by staying away." Wade was set on the idea.

"It's the reason we all stay away," Shan corrected. "I think it's pointless to keep pretending the warlords can't see what Mac is."

"Did Harlan say that?" Lambert asked.

"No. If he doesn't, Kaden does. I couldn't pry the details out of him, but I will. It bothers me." In truth, Kaden put her on-edge. She couldn't swear he was an Altered, even knowing he was. "We're screwing around out here, and it could put Mac in danger."

"How much concern?" Wade asked.

"I talk to Mac, he's been warned. Concerned enough that I mentioned it, but not so much that I'm prepared to do anything."

"Yet," Lambert added.

"What have you heard?" Wade asked.

"Same as Shan, there's something more than what we've stirred up on purpose. I'm not like you, but I'm not blind to what's going on."

Wade sighed. "Work with Harlan," he told Shannon.

"I'm the only one getting a head start on this. I should tell you two to get busy or go home," Shan let them know she was keeping tabs.

"Speaking of, what do we do about them?" Wade meant their cohorts watching an old television show being transmitted over a local station. Platte River had two, both on the air at various times during the day. They also had a short-range radio station that was on overnight and at the top of every hour with news and events.

"I'm not in a position to be giving orders," Lambert said. "Either of you can send them home."

"I didn't say we should send them home. I'm asking, when we get to the end of these negotiations, what would be the best course of action for them?"

"Do we have any new orders from Command?" Lambert asked.

"To keep in contact," Wade said. "The usual."

"I don't talk to The Vista," Shan said.

"The day we left Cody, we'd heard nothing new," Lambert agreed. "That's as technical and up-to-date as I've got. We kept radio silence on orders. So, no news is good news."

"Let's hope it stays that way," Shan said. "That's what they need to do. Call home for further instructions, or something. I mean Cody."

Lambert smiled and raised his bottle of beer in a toast. "Of course."

"We can talk about the actual reasons we're out here, or we can keep drinking," Wade said.

"We can do both," she suggested.

Wade sat back and let them discuss. One of his enhanced abilities was to absorb details. He'd been in overdrive for a few days running. Fatigued wasn't close to what he felt.

"If we're so damned smart, and so damned unique," Shan started, taking another healthy swig of the dark beer. "Why do all these people know our business? I mean, details. They know things no one outside The 'Conda..." She stopped, running things over in her mind.

"Don't leave us in suspense," Wade urged.

She blinked, losing focus. "Are you there?"

"Sometimes you get ahead of me."

Lambert understood what was happening and did nothing but listen. Both of their seconds were sitting in the next room if he needed help.

"We've given quite a few people free run over things we know. Things about us, The Vista, and now, all of this. We've worked on the assumption that if someone were interested in us, for any reason, it would be us they contacted."

"By 'contact', do you mean shooting us in the back, if they get the opportunity?" Wade said, painting a vivid picture in her thoughts. "If we get the chance, it might not be a bad idea to go over reports of incidents, at least from when we joined Security, where officers were targeted."

Shan was still dwelling on the idea. "I'm certain DeTessa is using Taylor to get information."

"Which Taylor?" Lambert asked.

"One," Wade answered. "Kyle told me she had a private talk with him."

"About me," Shan narrowed her gaze, peering inside at them.

"About a lot of things. She knows you are twins. She's right that we are catalysts for each other," Wade said.

"If you stop putting things in my head like the Junction," she chastised Wade. "I could tell you." The bloody ambush hadn't let her go a week without nightmares, two years on. "I know where our info leak is, and it's Taylor. Years, not days. He's been talking to DeTessa since right after the Blackout."

Wade's second, and he was starkly aware of how correct she was. Silence.

Then, "Are they tracking you through him?" Lambert asked her.

"No."

"Right now, we're like a neon sign to those who can see us. They got here when you got here," Wade nodded at Shan. "That's fine; that's what we intended. We see how fast they can be onto us. We can at least partially mask ourselves."

"After that show out on the interstate, they've seen how serious we can be," Lambert added. "We were exercising restraint."

"All things being considered, this is why I can't go home. Yes, I mean The Vista. The same is true for Mac and Shan. Argue all you want about it, but now it's obvious. Now, we have proof."

"What about our families?" she asked.

"They come to Cody to see us, or Black Hills if Shan can coax Harlan into an agreement. Safer for them, even with the travel. The Vista is more secure when we aren't there. In Cody, we have extra precautions, extra security. Black Hills isn't a place we're associated with."

"We're still missing something," Shan said.

"Yeah, what are we going to do about Taylor?" Wade agreed, standing to go add another log to the chimenea. He knocked on the glass of the double doors that led inside, pointed when they all looked up, and returned to his seat. "We might have another leak. Let's just ask."

It was a surprise when Hunter emerged, coat shrugged on. "What can I do for you?"

"Question," Wade warned. "Have you ever fed information about The Vista, Team Three, Security, or any aspect of our lives, to Senator Caulder, other Assembly members, the Vista Council, Command, or anyone else, without our prior consent?"

"No, never." He'd gotten used to questions that might insult other people.

"I'm satisfied with that," Wade sounded disappointed, while he was actually relieved. Asking Shan was pointless. She wouldn't have been wandering the outlands with him if there had been any doubt of his loyalties. He'd made a point to Hunter by asking. "Send Taylor One out, please."

He nodded and left. If there was one thing he was glad for in all of this, it was that he didn't understand what the hell they were talking about half the time.

Taylor joined them next.

"Hunter says he's not spying on us," Wade told him. "I believe him. Are you spying on us?"

Folding his arms, Taylor said, "Could you be more specific?"

Wade thought he was being sarcastic for a moment.

Shannon didn't. "More to the point, who are you working with, and why?"

"We all understand there's no point in my attempting to lie to you. The 'why' is complicated. Who, to the point, are the warlords. You've been mistaking them for the Sixth."

"Through Kaden," Wade said.

"No," Taylor answered. "Through DeTessa."

"Why?" Wade repeated.

"The easy version. They are aware of a third Altered; they've known about him as long as they've known about you. So did Rafe, so does Vance. They're almost certain it's Mac."

There was stark silence again.

Wade rubbed his eyes. "Rafe came after the team. They identified that there were two active Altered and suspected another. They look at him and think, 'maybe'. I can tell them it's me. Then they look right past me, and still can't see it."

"You had no permission to endanger us like that," Shan told Kyle. "No warning, no plan."

"I've been trying to keep Mac alive until this all fell together."

"He doesn't need your help. If you can call this fucking mess help." She was furious, more because he'd lied than what he'd done.

"Let's say Vance knows about Mac, and pretty much everyone in the western hemisphere knows we're here. That leads to Vance knowing where Mac is." Wade said.

"I don't know," Shan said. "Rafe couldn't see him."

"Was he stronger than Vance?" Lambert asked.

"In seeing other Altered, yes. Vance isn't like us."

"But Rafe was?"

Shan stared at him for a moment. "Don't ask things you don't want to hear the answer to."

"Hang on to that thought for a moment," Wade said, dismissing Taylor. "We'll have more questions about you and the warlords." Once he'd retreated inside, Wade continued. "We recognized there were other forces at work, and as of two years ago, we found out for certain not all of them were confined to The Vista. My opinion, we stay. We have plans in motion that took us a year to execute."

"We're never going to have this element of surprise again," Lambert agreed.

"DeTessa is why I'm here," Wade said. "That hasn't changed."

"I'm not worried about Mac," Shan said.

"Vance is going to react sooner or later."

"I'll let you in on a little secret," Lambert offered. "If it gets him out of Estes Park, he can disappear, and Skolkovo won't have anyone to blame."

"Is that part of this grand plan?" Shan asked.

"No," Wade spoke up. "It's not. If the opportunity arises, and he comes out of Colorado, I'll take care of it."

"We can't be planning this. He isn't Rafe, we can't prove he's done a thing to us." Shan was considering the repercussions later from Command.

"You forget I'm not in Command, and we're not planning a thing."

"I can't forget. I will never forget what happened..." she began, an idea taking over before she could finish the sentence. "That's why they keep looking at us like we're lying to them."

"We haven't been completely truthful with anyone recently," Lambert pointed out.

"Strong emotion blocks out other Altered from reading us. When we went into Manitou Springs, I used the most vivid image I had, when Wade blanked my memory, and again later, when it came back, to keep Rafe from seeing what we were doing."

"The Junction," Lambert figured.

"Close," Wade said. "On the way to the hospital, Mac flat-lined."

"Kaden could sense it later, others, too. That's why everyone is looking at us sideways. They consider our third Altered to be dead. Harlan does, Kaden told him, and others are going to think the same," Shan said.

"We spent too much time in Estes Park. Vance might consider the odds good enough to act."

"What do we do about Vance?"

"I've already told you," Wade said. "In the meantime, nothing has changed. Our plans haven't changed, and we'll institute our own security watch. They know we're expecting them, and that we aren't the easy prey we used to be."

"With this being neutral ground, the Elders will let them in, Vance's people, if they show up here waving a white flag." Shan was speculating about scenarios. "We're not invincible, and if anything, out here, we're vulnerable. Surrounded by strangers, in unfamiliar territory that belongs in part to Vance."

"We'll worry about it when we need to. Vance isn't stupid." Wade had his own ideas. "In the same light, it's probable that he has people here now. This is a trade route he shares with Angelfire. I can still see him coming after us, out in the open of neutral territory. It's no danger to him. Another possibility is that, out of spite or revenge, he tells the Angelfire Assembly what we are."

"Caulder already suspects it," Shan said.

"Which Caulder?"

"All of them," Lambert said. He'd heard things from Hunter, and about Hunter.

"I can handle the Angelfire Assembly," Shan decided.

"Good," Wade said. "If you have to go there as a retreat point, get word to someone in The 'Conda. We need to get Harlan to commit, and Cody will be set. Then we get ready for the summer."

Chapter Thirteen

Platte River night March 20

"We've been working on a few ideas about contacting Skolkovo," Harlan made conversation while they waited for Shannon. "Our previous attempts yielded no results, but things changed."

The kitchen was tiny, neat, and yet he would have known she stayed there, even if it was his first time stopping by. A stack of old paperback books sat on the counter next to her twin Sig 9mms and a pair of worn mirrored sunglasses.

Hunter offered him a beer, and he declined. "She's talking to Cody Base, so it may be a few minutes. They were supposed to have a video conference last night. There were power problems at the other end."

"Are you curious about those conversations, or does she tell you everything?"

"She tells me what she needs to, and that's the way I prefer our relationship."

Harlan wondered what he wasn't saying. He might ask later. The

About the Author

S. A. Hoag is an author, artist, amateur astronomer ("I just look at the stars, I can't tell you their names."), hockey fan, and accidental desert-dweller. Born in the middle of the Rocky Mountains of Colorado, she has lived in a number of cities, in a number of states, and is off on another adventure when not writing or painting. Science Fiction has always been her first interest in reading and writing. Many other genres sneak into the novels and that's all right with her.

Find her books at www.topaz08.com